HIS HUMAN WARD

MONSTERS LOVE CURVY GIRLS #5

MICHELE MILLS

Copyright © 2021 by Michele Mills

All rights reserved.

No part of this book may be reproduced in any form or by any electronic or mechanical means, including information storage and retrieval systems, without written permission from the author, except for the use of brief quotations in a book review.

Cover Artist: Mayhem Creations

Edits: Aquila Editing

* Created with Vellum

There are two ways of spreading light: to be the candle or the mirror that reflects it.
-Edith Wharton

1

THAYNE

"I have a human ward?"

I lean back in my chair, dumbfounded at this declaration. Hot smoke wafts from my nostrils as I assess the gravity of the situation.

A ward?

A human child has been left behind for *me* to care for? How can this be happening? I am Thayne Ashmoor, the Marquis of Ashmoor Manor. My ancestry traces back to the first fires of Tarvos. Anonymous children of random species aren't dumped upon the doorstep of a Hyrrokin fire lord.

The older, no-nonsense lawyer who arrived this morning from the Department of Children and Families gazes upon me with steady determination, ready to continue her bad news. "Yes, you have a—"

I slam a fist on my antique ebony desk. "How is that possible? Do you know who I am?"

Her eyes dart around the wood paneled room, scanning the many oil paintings of my illustrious ancestors. "Well, I…"

"There has to be a mistake," I growl. "No human in their right mind would leave a child for the Fire Lord of Ashmoor to raise.

How would a human even know who I am and how to contact your department on Tarvos? I don't know any humans." I wave a claw. "Well, except for that human who became the bound of my neighbor, Skoll Strikestone, but she's—"

"I know, I agree that it does seem strange," the lawyer sighs with resignation. She taps on her tablet. "I was surprised at first too. But I have an explanation for this odd chain of events." Her black eyes narrow. "Your great-uncle, the Fire-Baron Targek Ashmoor, left the planet two decades ago?"

"Yes…" I clench my fists. My tail twitches along the edge of my chair. Dammit. Targek is the long-lost black fish of our family. This has to be his fault. "Targek Ashmoor originally left Tarvos to perform a pilgrimage of Salo," I agree, "but never returned. My office has received the occasional message from him over the years, letting us know he's alive, but that's all. No one knows where he lives or what he's doing."

"Your great-uncle was apparently enamored of humans and decided to make New Earth his home. His bound was a human female."

"New Earth?" I grimace, horrified at the thought of an Ashmoor choosing to live on such a backwater planet among beings who could not flash-flame. "He's been living with humans for almost two decades? Are you saying that my great-uncle died recently?"

"Yes," she answers. "I'm sorry for your loss. He was living alone at the end because his bound died last moon cycle. He passed away peacefully in his sleep from a heart defect due to advanced age. A cleaning bot found him and notified the New Earth authorities. The human authorities seem to think he gave up living after his bound's sudden death."

I purse my lips, wondering if the humans on New Earth properly disposed of his body in accordance with Hyrrokin preparations for the afterlife. I make a quick note to ensure that Targek's remains are transferred to the Ashmoor family mausoleum. "He left stipulations that I raise his child?" I question.

"Well, actually he left provisions for you to care for his grandchild. It's all right here in Targek Ashmoor's will." A pink-tipped claw again taps on her tablet. "I am right now sending it to you so you can—"

How is this happening? A throbbing pain starts at my temples. "Forward the will to my butler, Barnabas Blackstone," I hiss. "He'll alert my personal lawyer."

"Oh…okay."

"This…this grandchild that I'm supposed to care for is half-Hyrrokin and half-human?"

"No, she's fully human. Your great-uncle adopted his bound's human child from a prior mating as his own offspring. Fire-Baron Ashmoor and his human did not have their own biological offspring. The child he adopted and her progeny are therefore citizens of Tarvos."

I lift an eye ridge. "That's an odd loophole."

"Yes, it's very rare for humans to be citizens outside of a work visa or a Bound ceremony. But the fire-baron's human granddaughter is now his sole heir, and she is automatically a citizen of Tarvos. But she will not inherit his title and currency until she comes of age. He specifically left instructions in his will for his great-nephew, Thayne Ashmoor, the present Fire Lord of Ashmoor, to take over responsibility of this child until she turns twenty-one."

I lean back in my chair and dig my claws into the armrests. "How could that asshole do this to me? I've got businesses to run, and the rainy season starts next week. I don't have time for this. Why can't another human on New Earth care for this child? Why can't her parents take care of her?"

The lawyer's features soften. "The child is an orphan. Her father died when she was an infant and her mother passed away from a drug overdose one moon cycle ago."

I drum my claws against the desk. Dammit to hyro hell. She recently lost both her grandparents and her mother too? "Did you say this child is a female?"

"Yes. Her name is Charlotte Cruz."

I reach up and rub my fingers against my scalp next to my left horn. A child, in my home? My throat tightens. "I don't have any living offspring of my own, nor do I have nieces or nephews. The only children I ever see are the offspring of my staff or of the families who work my land. And those are at a distance." There are no children around for a reason—the tragic death of my own son remains much too fresh upon my mind.

"You can hire more staff to care for this child until it comes of age and is no longer your responsibility."

I blow out a smoky breath. The lawyer is right, and for some reason this logic calms me down. I can throw currency at this problem to make it easier. The human child can be cared for by others.

I stand and walk over to the window to gaze at the long expanse of gardens in front of the mansion. A large group of Hyrrokin are working on rebuilding mother's reflective pool today. It is being restored, at Strikestone's expense. My mother used to love taking her grandson for walks along the banks of that pool, teaching him how to arc flash-flames across the water.

It is still hard for me to believe my mother is gone. She died one year ago of sudden heart failure. My mind often plays tricks on me, thinking she's on an extended vacation to Perth and will return momentarily.

I brace a claw against the window frame and think again, too, of my beloved three-year-old son, whom I lost in the temple fire. The sound of his childish laughter and the exact color of his Ashmoor flames. His smile, the curve of his tail and the shine of his starter horns. I once had a bound and a son, and they were both taken from me on the same night. It happened three years ago but I still remember the pain as if it were yesterday. I've vowed to never go through this heartache again. I am not worthy to care for offspring. My brother can carry on the family name, not me. His future offspring will become my heirs. And if he doesn't have offspring, there are three other cousins who I can choose from to carry on the Ashmoor line. This has been done before and it can happen again.

My tail twitches in agitation. The care and feeding of this orphaned human child is indeed my responsibility as the head of the Ashmoor estate. The difference here is that this human is only a ward I am providing protection to, nothing more. I will not be her parent. There will be no need to see her daily. I could in fact make sure she's properly cared for but see little of her.

I can do this.

I'm ready to take on this assignment, but I'm still annoyed. How could Targek Ashmoor, after close to twenty years of no communication whatsoever, just drop this off on my lap? A message, letting me know of this possibility within his will would've been nice. My schedule is packed today with face-to-face meetings and vid calls. "I don't have time for any of this," I complain with a rhetorical statement of general annoyance.

"This doesn't have to happen immediately," the lawyer answers. "You can contact New Earth government concerning the child and then wait to bring her to Tarvos. I'm sure there will be a delay in her placement due to several layers of bureaucracy."

I let out a steaming snort because this "bureaucracy" is of no consequence to me. My first cousin is in charge of the Department of Immigration. I will simply ping her later and get this matter resolved. Worry nibbles at the edges of my consciousness. If Targek has left this child's care to me, there must be a reason. She's an orphan with no one to properly care for her. Maybe she needs to be immediately rescued from her home planet? "No," I tell the lawyer, "I will not take the easy way out and let this placement move slowly. I will leave for New Earth immediately and retrieve this child."

Her eyes widen.

"Barnabas?" I yell.

My butler instantly opens the office door and stands at the ready. He was probably listening to my every word, right outside in the hallway. This is exactly why I pay him an enormous amount of currency for his continued employment.

"I need to contact that organization Strikestone works for, immediately."

"Yes, my Lord." Barnabas answers as he steps forward and hands me a tablet. Strikestone's harsh face is already displayed on the screen. A smile widens across my features. My butler's efficiency never ceases to amaze me.

"Why is Barnabas pinging me?" Strikestone growls. "As if I have all the time in the universe to await your Lordship's pleasure?" His voice drips with sarcasm.

I get right to the point. "I was alerted to the fact that I have a human ward on New Earth. I am required to take possession of her immediately."

Skoll lets out a deep belly laugh. "The thirteenth Fire Lord of Ashmoor is going to be a guardian to a *human* child? Oh, that's a good one. This is going to be interesting." He turns his head and shouts, "Ariana? Ariana...? Oh hells, she's already left for the day. I'll have to tell her about this later; she can come by and give you advice about how to care for a human."

This is acceptable, so I nod in agreement. Having Skoll's human bound speak to the new staff I'll be hiring as well as having her help train the present staff on all things human *would* be helpful. "I don't know the exact coordinates of my new ward," I explain.

"Aaah. You want my team to find her for you?"

"Yes, I need her position triangulated as soon as possible so I can go to New Earth and retrieve her. I will bring her back to my domicile." I snap my claw at the lawyer. "Send the child's information immediately to Molten Lava Security."

Annoyance flashes across her features, but she taps on her tablet, doing my bidding.

Strikestone glances down at his own tablet. "Got it," he declares. "Let me get to work on this. I'll get back to you within the hour, probably less." And then the screen goes dark.

"Lord Ashmoor?" The lawyer stands and tries to regain my attention as I stride towards the exit. "The child won't be expecting you. You have no idea who she is living with or what those conditions are. Maybe you should contact the adults she is with first, and then wait a moon cycle to bring her over?"

"No, no time for that," I bark out. "If she's to live with me under my protection, then it will happen *now*... Barnabas?"

My butler hands me my formal sash that bears the Ashmoor coat of arms along with our family motto. I pull it over my head and down across my bare chest, as I've done every day of my life since I ascended to the position of fire lord. "Get a room ready in the nursery," I order. "Today I am retrieving a human child who will be living amongst us as my ward. Hire a nanny and a tutor."

He nods his head. "It will be so. I will alert housekeeping and the other staff to the child's arrival, and all will be ready upon your return. Your hovercraft is waiting for you out front, my Lord. The pilot will take you to the transporter station."

I leave the lawyer behind, knowing Barnabas will see her out. A porter opens the front door and I exit the manor and march down the stone steps. The morning air is crisp this time of year and I take a deep breath, trying to absorb what freshness I can until we're all homebound during the rainy season. I cross the long terrace at the front edge of the east wing and stride through the windy roar as the powered hovercraft awaits on the landing pad.

Jinos, the pilot, dressed in proper Ashmoor livery, lowers the ramp for me. I lift my chin in greeting and step up into the interior and settle into the luxurious back seat. Soon the door closes and we lift into the air and fly over the green expanse of my estate.

I pause to take out a glass and pour myself a finger of amber fire alcohol from the decanter and sip at it, soothing the tightness in my chest at the thought of another child suddenly in my life. There hasn't been a child living in my manor in close to three years.

Can I keep this one safe?

The great fire of '05 on the Ashmoor estate decimated the multigod temple and also took the lives of my bound and my son.

That fire was not an accident.

It was intentionally set by my former bound.

I swirl the liquid in the crystal cup and then throw back the last of it. We fly directly to the Tarvos transporter station and arrive within thirty-five minutes. The hovercraft lands on the roof and my tablet pings as I pound down the ramp. Strikestone has sent the coordinates to this child, Charlotte Cruz and all the info I'll need. Molten Lava has even included a map lock on the child's exact location that I can follow in real time. I smile with satisfaction. I will go immediately to some city named Singapore on New Earth, retrieve her, and then bring her back to Tarvos.

She will be safe, and my duty will be fulfilled.

And I will return to my work.

2

CHARLOTTE

I'm getting married today and I'm so freaking depressed.
"Charlotte? Charlotte Cruz? Pay attention," the seamstress grouses. "You should've eaten less yesterday. Well, really, you should've been on a strict diet for the last month in preparation for your wedding. Have you even *tried* to lose weight? I'm never going to be able to get this dress closed in the back."

The women here have been trying to fat shame me all day. The way their lips curl and the little remarks they make—my thick thighs and wide hips disgust them. There's a roll in my back under my bra and they think my boobs are big and messy. "You'd be so pretty if you lost weight," the designer sighs and clucks.

Is this supposed to be a compliment?

"There's nothing wrong with me," I try to say. Even though I'm not sure if I even believe what I'm saying. It's hard to find self-respect when literally everyone sends messages that they find your appearance lacking.

"Uh huh."

I shake my head. Like I care that my dress won't close? I've been so stressed I've actually been eating *more*. I recently discovered that my new best friend and my future mother-in-law both hate me and are only pretending to like me so they can steal my currency.

Yep.

It sucks. Anyone would be upset over that, right? And to make matters worse, my mom died last month from a drug overdose. We weren't close because my mom had morphed over the years into a drug addict who only cared about her next hit and absolutely nothing else. Not me, not life in general, nothing. This means I'm not as sad as I should be at finding out my own mother passed away, because she'd been very distant from me. The moment I graduated from my private girls school and moved out to live in university housing, I stopped speaking to her. I think she was relieved to be done with me too because she never tried to contact me. And that was almost two years ago. I was trying to make my way in the world, all by myself, like usual.

But it was still heartbreaking knowing my mother had died broke and alone in a whorehouse, trading sex for drugs. It was tragic. I wouldn't wish that type of life on anyone.

And then I received even more shocking news. Last week two peacekeepers and a New Earth Government lawyer showed up at my apartment to let me know of the recent death of my Hyrrokin adoptive grandfather? This male's wife, my biological grandmother, had also died in her sleep a month ago too. It was a stunning revelation—finding out I had two grandparents and also, finding out they'd both recently died. It turned out my mother never told me I had living grandparents who cared about me? I guess I shouldn't be too surprised. This type of behavior was exactly why I'd left her and never looked back.

I was served notice to arrive at the reading of the will. And that was how I discovered I was the sole heir to this male's fortune and he'd all along been watching me and helping me with scholarships. My grandparents were the mysterious benefactors who'd left me monthly stipends for housing and food.

And the barrier to my relationship with my grandparents was

my mom. She'd taken me away from them when I was little and made sure we never saw them.

The whole reason my mother kept me from my grandmother and grandfather was because she was completely freaked out by Targek's appearance. I do remember my mom telling me her mother had once remarried to a male who looked like the devil. But I'd thought she was joking. I didn't realize he literally looked like the devil because he wasn't human and those were the features of the Hyrrokin species. And she'd also told me they'd both died in a freak vehicular accident when I was a baby.

Yeah.

"Here, try on these shoes. I think they will look better than the other pair."

A whole team of women swirl around me, trying to make me look beautiful for my wedding, which is starting within the hour, and all I can think of is how to get out of this mess. I woke up this morning ready to exchange vows with my fiancé, despite the fact that last night I'd learned his sister was only pretending to be my best friend.

Maya and her mother both wanted to be in here with me this morning as I dressed for the wedding but I'd ordered them out. I think they were surprised to see me sticking up for myself like that, but...sometimes a girl is pushed too far.

I was really looking forward to this marriage as a new beginning. A fresh start. Well, it wasn't the be-all, end-all, but it sounded like a good idea. I could grow to love Jaden Johnson, right? Jaden was nothing but nice to me and so ridiculously handsome, how could I not want to be near him? I thought we got along well and laughed a lot. But I've learned that as far as Maya and her mother are concerned, my engagement was nothing more than a long con. And as each minute progresses this morning toward the procession down the aisle, the more I think I need out of this catastrophe.

"I can't stand her," I overheard Maya hiss last night as she talked on her tablet to a friend. "Charlotte's weight is disgusting. Have you seen how big she is now? And she wants us to spend our free time gardening or volunteering with poor kids. Can you believe? It's silly. I don't have time for this shit. I haven't been out clubbing in ages. Ugh. But she's going to be a rich bitch because she's the heir to some fortune from off planet and my mom says I have to do this so Jaden can marry her and we can all be rich bitches too."

This was the moment everything came crashing down. I stood in the hallway with my hand over my mouth, trying not to sob out loud. I wanted to ping Jaden and cry to him about what I'd heard…but I wasn't sure how he'd react. Maybe he'd known all along that Maya and his mom didn't like me but didn't want to tell me? Was he in on it too or was he embarrassed by their behavior?

I didn't know.

How could I be so stupid? My best friend was pretending to like me so her brother could have a rich wife. I guess I'd been so excited that someone as beautiful and popular as Maya Johnson would want to hang out with me, I'd ignored all the warning signs. Maya was the one who'd referred to us as "best friends."

There were red flags though, I'd just chosen to not see them.

I'd had a tiny crush on a nice guy from one of my classes. I'd admired his wickedly sharp sense of humor from afar, never approaching him because I'd figured nothing would ever come of something between a tall, thin guy like him and a big girl like me, so I hadn't even bothered to try. But one night I was pleasantly surprised to discover him holding hands and sharing passionate kisses with a girl I assumed was his girlfriend, and the most important part—she was overweight. It looked like we were of similar weight and shape. Her boobs were bigger than mine and her waist a little smaller, but similar. This gave me all kinds of hope for my future. Not hope that I'd steal him away from her, I'd never do anything like that, just hope that one day I could get "the guy" too. That maybe the weight I carried wasn't going to be a barrier to love and happiness like I sometimes thought it would, and that there was a man out there who could see past it.

Maya knew about my unrequited crush and had always told me it was silly and hopeless because he was way out of my league due to my weight.

I tapped her shoulder. "Look," I gushed, "Julio from art class is dating a girl who looks about the same weight as me. Isn't that cool? Maybe I could have a chance someday with someone, despite my size."

Maya turned and studied the couple from across the street. "No," she snorted, "you weigh a lot more than she does. You two don't even look the same."

"Oh."

"I mean, really, she's not as big as you at all. She's not. She's actually very pretty." And then Maya dismissed me and went back to flirting with the guy she'd just met, and I stood there, trying to not let the hurt show on my face.

"Lift your arms," the designer orders. I do as she instructs, and let the attendants lay the wedding dress over me and settle the layers of white skirt around and behind me.

And I wonder, does Jaden know his mom and sister are pretending to like me so they can try and take my currency? Is he in on all of this or are his sister and mother the masterminds? I haven't confronted him yet about what I learned. I haven't confronted anyone yet. I really, really hate confrontation. And I don't know if it's Jaden and me against his family and I need to help him get away from them, or if it's the three of them against me and I need to get out of here, quick.

I've never had any family of my own, and all the Johnsons were so welcoming. I guess I made excuses in order to have that extended family as my own? Maya was my new roommate this last semester at university and we became instant best friends. She learned I was alone and invited me to her home during school breaks. Her mom, Serena, was so amazing and welcoming. And Maya's older brother kept showing up, flirting with me and asking me out. I could not believe that this handsome black man, with perfect teeth, a smooth voice and wide shoulders would look at me twice. Jaden is a lawyer and about ten years older than me. A man, not a boy, with a real job.

Maya and her brother are both blessed with vid model good looks and their parents are stunning too. Hell, the entire family is so good-looking and gregarious they could seriously have their own reality vid show. Meanwhile, I'm thick, curvy, overweight and boring—nothing to write home about. My thin hair is in an easy-to-care-for bob; I wear little makeup and live mainly in baggy clothes because "comfort over fashion." I attend university full-time on a scholarship, tend to my container garden and watch lots of black-market original planet vid shows and read too many contraband romance ebooks. Mainly I putter around with my plants, study for my classes and tutor small children at the local school. I have a few friends from my botany club, but we aren't that close. One day I hope to be a landscape designer on another planet. I love the idea of learning all about how to grow plants on a variety of planets and conditions. My friends at university laugh at how much I want off planet to pursue my interests, because they consider it a fantasy. But if I'm going to dream, why not dream big?

My head was turned by Maya's handsome brother and how many times he told me I was "beautiful." And then I spent lots of time with his family and I was sucked in. Serena taught me how to cook Johnson family recipes. Maya and I studied together and went out to exclusive student parties I'd normally never know about. I sat at a long dinner table each Sunday night, like I was a member of their family, with all their aunts, uncles and cousins.

Damn they knew my weaknesses and went right for it. A girl who was alone, insecure about her looks and wishing she had the love of a boyfriend and an extended family. Bam, bam, they did a one-two punch and hit both of my weak spots. I fell for their attentions hook, line and sinker.

Jaden proposed to me at a family gathering. I was surprised when it happened because we'd only been dating for a month and had never spoken of marriage, and up to that point he'd only held my hand and given me a few chaste kisses on the lips. I'd been starting to wonder if we were better as friends rather than lovers. But his entire extended family and everyone he'd ever known had been gathered around us when he went down on bended knee with a beautiful ring in his hand, ready to slide onto my finger. I felt bad for him because the proposal was being livestreamed. Like, how could I say no and publicly embarrass him? And Jaden Johnson was great on paper, and I could grow to love him, right? Maybe he'd be willing to leave New Earth too someday?

Looking back, I should've said no despite the on-the-spot pressure. Being rushed into the proposal was part of the con too, wasn't it? Which makes me question Jaden's motives again.

"Okay, hold your breath. We're going to make this work." The women tighten the old-fashioned corset they've put around my waist, which is recently back in fashion for some bizzarro reason. And now I'm barely breathing. Finally, the back is fastened, and I'm shoved into the dress.

"It's beautiful," someone sighs. "Even if she's a big girl, it's still a beautiful dress. You've done an amazing job, succeeding in making this bride look beautiful."

I roll my eyes as everyone hugs and congratulates the designer for managing to make the fat girl (me) look pretty despite my obvious flaws. It's ridiculous. They talk around me like I'm not even there.

I place my hand against my stomach and try to take a full breath.

"The price we pay for fashion," the designer quips.

"Fashion before comfort!" another woman chirps.

A full-length mirror is propped on the wall and I stare at myself as the women continue to chatter around me. They're packing up all their supplies, readying to leave.

The bridal gown is exquisite. The dress has a long train and there's pretty, sheer veil that falls over my face. But I feel like any minute I'm going to poke someone's eye out with the possibility of exploding cleavage. The dress is nothing I would've picked out for myself. I'd rather wear something loose and short. And maybe be able to stand barefoot and relaxed. That would be nice.

I let out a breath.

Why *am* I getting married to Jaden? Why am I still going through the motions of this wedding?

I don't love this guy. His sister and mom hate me.

And…and I found out at the reading of the will that I'm a future multi-millionaire. Targek Ashmoor was a very wealthy Hyrrokin fire-baron and in one more year I'll inherit his fortune and his title. I'm going to go from university student, living on a stipend, to sudden wealth? To be truthful it's a little scary. I don't know anything about managing money at that scale. But my adoptive grandfather, who wasn't even human, left me this fortune in his will. I learned I had caring grandparents—one biological and one adoptive—who I wasn't in contact with but had designated me to be their sole heir. It's still shocking. I had no idea. But I guess I won't come into the inheritance for another year because it won't be available to me until I'm of age, according to Hyrrokin law.

"Okay, let's get you out there," the wedding planner says with a breezy attitude as she hands me my bouquet of flowers. "The ceremony is about to start."

They open the door to the dressing room and I make my way down the hallway to stand at the doors that are about to open so I can walk down the aisle the moment the music starts. I glance over at Jaden's female "cousins" who are lining the walls. They glare at me for a second before hiding their anger and jealousy behind fake smiles of encouragement. My mind flashes to images of times I've thought these same women were all hugging Jaden a bit too tight and kissing him too close to his lips. I once saw the curvy blonde one grabbing his ass... And it hits me hard —these women aren't his family, they're his girlfriends. His groupies. He's been having sex with these women all along, hasn't he?

They snort and giggle behind me as the doors open and the music starts. I walk down the aisle alone, processing all the lies. My nose stings and hot tears burn behind my eyes. He's in on it too. Jaden is only marrying me for my money. It's sad but true.

I'm ninety-nine percent certain that my groom, as well as his family, somehow knew all along that I was coming into this fortune and that's why they befriended me in the first place.

None of this is what I ever wanted. My engagement ring is enormous because Jaden picked it out for me. My groom is evil personified, and I was tricked into this doomed marriage by him and his family.

I'm seconds from breaking into a full-on ugly cry at the enormity of this farce. I can't believe how elaborate it is. My tiny group of university friends from botany club sit bravely on my side of the chapel and give me wide, genuine smiles. But mainly they sense how upset I am, and they start to frown with worry.

I continue down the aisle and notice that one half of the church is full to bursting with Jaden's family and friends. Maya and her mother are in the front row with fake smiles. Jaden looks so very handsome in his black suit and tie that perfectly matches my pink flowers. Ugh. I met all of these people just three months before I found out I had a long-lost grandfather. How did they know about him?

My throat tightens as I step onto the altar. I face my groom and slide off my engagement ring. I'm kinda mad at myself for letting this happen to me. Here I am, being swindled by people who don't care about me. And they all slipped in so easily. All my boundaries were laid bare and disintegrated. I felt weak and powerless, which isn't a good feeling.

"Charlotte? What's wrong?" my groom questions with fake concern.

Rage begins to replace the hurt and despair. I let out a low growl and toss the ring at his chest. It bounces off and hits the floor.

I'm going to *publicly* let Jaden, his mom, my so-called best friend, and Jaden's "girlfriends" know exactly what I think of them and their scam.

No fucking way am I marrying this guy.

3

CHARLOTTE

And right then, as if by magic, the church doors burst open. I turn my head at the sound. A bare-chested, red-skinned male with tall black horns is marching into the sanctuary. He's obviously not of this world.

Women scream and children scramble as a huge satanic-looking, monstrous being stomps down the aisle, flicking his black barbed tail. Security guards yell out and rush him, like he's an intruder. He's flashing flames over everyone's heads and wreaking chaos in his wake.

Why is this guy here? I don't know, but I sniff away my tears, a smile widening across my face. This male is Hyrrokin, which is the same species as my adoptive grandfather who recently passed away. Is this some sort of connection to my inheritance?

Also, I'm secretly glad the wedding ceremony is obviously over.

He looks right at me. A shiver of anticipation runs up my spine as this Hyrrokin makes his way up the aisle.

Two different women scream and faint at his appearance. He's snarling and blasting flame from his distended jaw. This male is crashing my wedding, but I don't mind. He's not actually hurting anyone. Curtains, cushions and other flammable property are bursting into flame, but still, no one appears hurt, he's just keeping everyone out of his way.

I look around and notice I'm the only one still standing up front because everyone else evacuated. The priest, the bridesmaids, the groomsmen—all gone. The front pews are empty now. I have no idea where Jaden went.

The huge red Hyrrokin makes his way down the aisle, stomps up onto the altar and stands right in front of me, taking the place of my absent groom. He's barefoot and bare-chested but wears a nice pair of black trousers and a black belt with a heavy silver buckle. His black barbed tail juts in the air behind him.

I lift my chin, continuing to stare at him through my veil. My fingers tighten around my wedding bouquet. Holy gods, he's so very tall and wide.

He glances down at the glass tablet he's carrying in his left hand, which is tipped with silver claws. The tablet starts blinking red. And then I realize he's been using a locator to find me. I'm his target. He reaches forward, delicately pinches the bottom of my sheer veil and carefully lifts it up and over the back of my head. He stares down at my face. "Charlotte Cruz?" the devil questions.

I give a jerky nod, shocked into silence. He's so close. So massive. He looks me up and down. His lethal gaze lingers on my chest and my cheeks heat. Butterflies take off in my belly, because under the black sash that lies diagonally across his chest is a six-pack of red-skinned abs and the beginning of the V leading down the sides of his muscular hips. The red, black and silver color combo looks cool as hell, literally. He's barefoot and his toes are tipped with deadly silver claws. And yet somehow, I find him sexy?

His brow furrows underneath the two huge, shiny black horns that burst out from either side of his forehead. "I have learned today that according to Targek Ashmoor's will, you are now my ward," he announces with an impossibly deep voice and a flash of white fangs. "And I am your legal guardian. I'm here to take you with me back to Tarvos."

"I'm your *what*? I'm going where?"

Then the monster grunts in response, sweeps me off my feet and carries me away from the altar. I let out a squeak of surprise.

Two more guards try to rush up the aisle to block his exit. The devil doesn't even break stride. He lifts his head, cracks open his jaw again and sends another flame in the air, high above me and over the heads of the two guards. They scream and run away.

I don't even bother to argue at how I'm being carried away by this deadly Hyrrokin. I view him as my savior—the being who stopped the wedding that needed to end anyway. I wrap my arms around his corded neck and hold on tight as he kicks open the doors.

"Charlotte? Charlotte?" a voice shrieks from behind me. "Don't worry. I'll come for you. I'll save you. We're still going to get married."

I turn my head, look over the Hyrrokin's shoulder and spy Jaden hiding behind the altar.

Uh huh. Nope, not gonna happen. Even if I really was in trouble, which I'm not, there's no way Jaden is going to save me. That man's a coward. He's never served in any kind of military a day in his life. He's never so much as thrown a punch or held a weapon. He golfs all day long with his buddies on a public holodeck while driving in a cart and paying for a caddy.

I give him a smug smile and a little wave of my fingers. The doors clang shut behind me, and he's gone. Gone from my life forever.

Thank gods.

I blink into the bright sunlight as we exit the church and I smile wide, thankful to be out of that situation. I tug at the veil and pull it off the top of my head and toss it over my shoulder. A group of young women are gawking at us, so I toss my bouquet to them. They squeal with delight and race for it. I giggle as one of them snatches it from the others and hugs it to her chest.

Then I wrap both my hands again around the devil's thick neck. I love touching his warm skin. "Where did you say we are going?"

"Tarvos. I'm taking you to Tarvos," the Hyrrokin rumbles as we head towards the curb. His black horns glimmer in the sunshine and two sharp fangs peek past his sexy black lips. He continues to easily carry me in his arms as if I weigh nothing, not even remotely appearing out of breath. "We're leaving right now and going to my home planet."

"Oh wow. Right now? But…"

"Yes," he answers firmly, then stops in front of a very fancy-looking auto drive. "We are leaving right now." A door slides open. He bends down, places me in the spacious back seat and I scoot over, trying my best to arrange my skirt and train as he enters behind me.

We both settle in our seats and the door closes and the auto-drive takes off. That easy. I turn around and look out the window behind us as we pull away from the curb. I hear the muffled sound of a fire alarm. People are standing outside of the church and smoke is billowing out of the doors and windows. Fire-drones are arriving to put out the fire. Oops.

"My name is Thayne Ashmoor," he tells me. "You may call me Thayne."

I reach forward and offer my hand to the male who saved me from a doomed marriage. He claps my palm inside his large red fingers and I give him a brilliant smile. "And I am Charlotte Cruz," I answer with a firm handshake. "It's nice to meet you. Thank you for what you did for me back there. I'm grateful." I'm in a giddy mood because I was swooped up by a very muscular male and carried away from the altar in my time of need. And he was shooting fire out of his mouth, which was pretty amazing. Like something out of a show on the vid channels. How can this possibly be my real life? "You said we're leaving to go to Tarvos?" I'm surprisingly unperturbed at the thought of leaving for another planet. Maybe because it's always been a secret dream of mine to go off planet?

"Yes. I live on Tarvos. It is the home planet for the Hyrrokin species."

"Oh, okay. But, oh no, I...I don't have any luggage," I tell him. "The only clothes I have are what I'm wearing." I figure we're driving to the Singapore Space Dock so we can travel off planet on a spaceship. I was planning on leaving today anyway to start my honeymoon, so I'm not as freaked out at the idea of leaving the planet in a hurry as someone else would. My neighbor is set to watch my apartment and most of my personal items are boxed because I was going to move in with Jaden.

"You don't need your luggage. I will purchase whatever you require."

I lean back in the seat and notice that Thayne is still holding my hand and I don't mind at all. "I'm trying to figure out why you're here. I assume your arrival has to do with the estate of Targek Ashmoor? Did you say back there that I'm your ward? And you think you're my...?"

"I'm your guardian and you're my ward. Targek designated me as your legal guardian and I'm here to take you with me to the planet Tarvos. You are going to live with me in my domicile and I will care for you until you are of age."

This is getting weirder. "Of age? What does that mean? I guess I thought you were taking me to Tarvos to visit but you want me to permanently move to your planet? This has to be a mistake. You can see I'm not a child. I don't exactly need a guardian. Are you sure you're supposed to take *me* to Tarvos? I'm...I'm worried you have the wrong human. It would be terrible for us to both travel for weeks aboard a space liner, get all the way to your home planet and then find out I'm the wrong human."

He snorts out a puff of smoke. "I'm certain you are the correct human. And we aren't using a space liner to return home. We are using a transporter to return to Tarvos, then switching to my personal hovercraft the rest of the way to Ashmoor Manor. We'll be at my domicile within the hour."

My mouth drops open. "Oh wow." I glance again at the sash on his chest which I now realize has an elaborate crest of some sort. His belt buckle is extra shiny, and his trousers do seem to be of the finest material and cut. "Are you the King of Tarvos?"

He lets out a deep belly laugh. "No, I'm not actual royalty, but the queen is my second cousin. I am the thirteenth Fire Lord of Ashmoor. Your grandfather was my great-uncle. Is there a problem?"

"No, I've just never known anyone who could afford a transporter before, so I'm a little flustered."

"Heh." He squeezes my hand. "Tell me, what was that gathering of humans back there? You're covered with so much pinching fabric and there were many humans collected into that building. Why were you standing up front and they were all staring at you?"

And then I realize he has no idea. "It was my wedding."

"Wedding? What is that?"

"Well, that's why that man was yelling about how he would come and try and find me. He and I were about to get married."

"Married? I recognize that word. That is a human Bound ceremony. You were about to become that male's mate? You are old enough to become a bound?"

"Yes, of course I am."

"Do you want me to return you to him so you can claim him as your bound?" Thayne Ashmoor says with a scary voice.

"No. No, I hate him. That whole ceremony was a mistake. I'm happy we're driving away."

He grunts. "Good…I originally thought I was coming to New Earth to retrieve a young child and take that girl with me back to Tarvos. How old are you?"

No wonder his gaze was lingering on my chest when the blinking red light first led him to me. My curves must've been a shock. "I'm nineteen years old but I turn twenty next week. How old do I need to be on Tarvos to legally be considered an adult?"

"Twenty-one. At twenty years old you are old enough to vote and mate, but you are not a legal citizen with full rights until you turn twenty-one."

"Oh, well at least you'll only need to be in charge of me for a little over a year. That's not so bad. And you don't really need to look after me. As you can see, on New Earth I'm considered an adult. I'm used to taking care of myself. I could live separately from you on Tarvos if you'd like. All you'd have to do is check in on me, through a tablet. This doesn't have to be a big deal, right?"

"No," he says with authority. "You're staying with me in my domicile until you come of age. You will learn Hyrrokin customs and receive an implant for our language. It is only right that you learn about the Ashmoors from whence your inheritance stems."

And right then I realize we've been speaking English this whole time. This means this male went through the bother of getting an implant of my language before he arrived so he could speak with me. How sweet. "I agree that visiting the planet of the grandfather I never knew and learning his history is only right. But I can't stay there and live permanently."

"You can," he declares.

I crook an eyebrow at him. He continues to stare at me, waiting for me to try to contradict him.

The auto drive stops at the transporter station. I've never been here before, so I eagerly lean forward to stare through the window in amazement at the fancy architecture. Transporter trips are normally much too expensive for a mere mortal such as myself to even contemplate. Jaden and I weren't even planning on using the transporter for our honeymoon because we couldn't afford it.

Thayne opens the door to the auto drive and steps out, then

he reaches back, takes my hand and helps me out too. I step out and fluff out my skirts. "I promise I don't normally dress this formal," I say, trying to explain my OTT outfit. "This was made specifically for my mating ceremony."

He frowns at my gown then grabs ahold of my hand and pulls me along with him to the station. In seconds my high heels click along the shiny floors of the main entrance. People scream at the sight of Thayne as we traverse through the lobby. I think they're worried he's kidnapping me? Security guards eye us and talk into their communication units. Thayne doesn't seem to even notice the commotion he's causing. Probably because he's on New Earth for only a nanosecond, to retrieve me, and I'm sure he assumes he'll never return. Plus, we're only *humans*. We're considered primitive and of no consequence to the other citizens in the four sectors.

"I'm truly grateful for what you did back there," I pant from behind him, trying to keep up with his longs strides as well as remind my new "guardian" that I think he's pretty awesome.

"What did I do?" he asks as we turn a corner into a smaller hallway.

A chuckle escapes my lips. Again, he has no idea. "You saved me from having to publicly say no to that man, and somehow make it out of there despite the crowd. It was going to be messy. My fiancé was trying to trick me into marrying him just so he could steal my inheritance."

A growl rumbles in his chest as he lets go of my hand and opens the door to our specific transportation room. "I will return and kill that human for you," he says matter-of-factly.

I walk inside and place a hand on his veiny forearm because I can't refrain from touching him. I miss being held in his massive arms and I also miss the feel of his rough claw holding my fingers. "No. Don't worry about him. I don't want you to get in trouble. He's not worth the effort."

Thayne Ashmoor narrows his eyes and gives me a curt nod.

The moment we enter our transporter room, a chorus of wails and shrieks ensues. Uh oh. The staff completely freaks out over the arrival of a Hyrrokin in their midst. Their reaction is nearly as bad as the prior chaos in the chapel. Employees literally run and hide. A girl is openly weeping, and I feel bad for her.

I grab Thayne's hand to try and show the others he's harmless. Smoke wafts from his nostrils at his annoyance with the delay. This doesn't help matters. He really does look terrifying.

I squeeze his palm. "Be nice and let me do the talking, okay?"

A growl rumbles in his chest, but he lets me take the lead.

I pluck our tickets from his other claw, hand them over to the nearest attendant and explain who we are and that Thayne isn't "the devil incarnate, or Satan himself" as they've been screeching. "Thayne Ashmoor isn't trying to kidnap me," I explain to the guards who just arrived with blasters ready. "I'm happily leaving the planet with him. He's simply a Hyrrokin from the planet Tarvos who wants me to return to his home planet with him, and the sooner you get us on a transporter disk, the quicker we'll leave."

The employees immediately calm down. The guards holster their weapons. The girl behind the counter wipes her eyes, blows her nose and then in a shaky voice begins listing the safety rules.

4

THAYNE

I can't believe how beautiful this human female is.
    I had no idea humans could be so exotic and fantastically gorgeous at the same time. Prior to this trip to New Earth, I'd barely known humans existed.

Charlotte speaks pleasantly to the transporter staff in a way they understand, causing them to stop screaming and do her bidding, and I'm enthralled at her take-charge attitude. My new ward is a fully-grown, sexy, gorgeous, unmated human female whose husky voice reminds me of sweaty encounters and tangled bedsheets. How is this possible? I'd thought I was traveling to this backwater planet to rescue a young child in need of care, but instead I find this luscious adult female is my ward?

She wears some sort of clothing with layers upon layers of white fabric that unfortunately cover her arms and shoulders from my gaze. It puffs out to a skirt that brushes the ground. This dress is odd. But even so, I can see her figure is lush. Her thick waist is the perfect size for me to wrap my large claws around. My forked tongue could lick the globes of her large breasts. She has a full ass that I want to grab and hold from behind while I watch my large cock slowly sink into her wet channel. The moment I saw her I was instantly attracted to her. She lacks horns and claws and doesn't even have a tail, nor can she flash-flame. And yet I still find her incredibly sexy.

And I scented her own arousal for me in return, the moment I met her at the gathering place of humans.

On New Earth she is considered an adult, but on Tarvos she is underage and therefore in my care. I cannot follow through with any of my explosive pleasure mating urges. It is both illegal and unethical. A growl rumbles in my chest as I pause to message my pilot, letting him know I will arrive with my ward momentarily and to ready the hovercraft.

The humans in the room calm down and gesture for us to step onto the nearest light disks. I stand next to my ward who is now on her own matching disk. She gives me a tremulous smile, exposing blunt teeth. And that's when I notice her skin isn't truly colorless but has a golden glow that I enjoy.

When has a fire lord ever been confronted with such a dilemma? I haven't felt this type of hot lust for a female since before my arranged Bound Ceremony. Actually, this is the most enflamed I've been for a female in my entire life.

This isn't good.

Charlotte Cruz is only nineteen but will turn twenty in seven diurnals. This means for the next week she is legally underage. When she turns twenty years old, she'll be old enough to mate and have offspring, but still won't be considered an adult with all the full rights of a Hyrrokin citizen until she turns twenty-one. Thus, she will remain my ward for one more year.

I will be in charge of a sexy, adult female I desperately want to pleasure mate for a whole planetary rotation? She will be living with me at Ashmoor Manor and one week from now she will legally be of age to mate.

Oh hells.

The hum of the transporter fills the room.

We are very close, and her lovely scent of blossoms and

sunshine tickles my nose. She smiles at me and I can again smell her arousal. My cock thickens in my trousers. The moment we met on the altar and she looked me up and down, I scented the light waft of her arousal. The scent increased as we entered the enclosed space of the auto drive. She wants me as much as I want her. I want to bury my face in the crook of her neck and inhale. If she weren't forbidden—if she were Hyrrokin, unmated, nearer to my age and not in my care—I would be arriving at the manor and dragging her to my room to place her on my red dick. That's how much I want to pleasure mate her. But instead, I must keep my epic lust at bay.

This will be difficult.

The countdown ends and a tickle starts in my stomach as the transportation process begins. Our atoms painlessly separate and shoot across the four sectors. The two of us instantly reform on matching light disks at the Tarvos transporter station.

My eyes blink open in darkness until the temporary blindness recedes, and then I see the smiling, familiar faces of the Hyrrokin transporter staff. I smile in return because it's good to be home. Their deep red features and black horns bring me comfort. New Earth was a chaotic mess. Nervous humans constantly shouting and rushing to get away from me. I shake my head and let out a snort of disgust.

I reach out and claim Charlotte's tiny hand in my own. This is her first time using this type of technology and she's never before left her home planet. I step close and place a claw on the small of her back. "Female, are you well?"

She gazes up at me with sparkling brown eyes laced with a flecks of green. All humans have a strange amount of follicles on the top of their heads and I find that Charlotte's brown "hair," which ends at her shoulders, is shiny and sweet-smelling and I want nothing more than to run my claws through it and see how it feels. My eyes drop and follow the curve of her full lips to the slope of her jaw and along the length of her neck to the white fabric that blocks my view of the rest of her curves and golden skin. I will be pleased when she is no longer in this human mating dress and instead wears typical Hyrrokin clothing.

My human ward looks at the transporter staff in the room and lets out a squeak of distress. She grabs onto me, digging her nails into my forearm. I draw her close and brush my lips against her ear. "Female, we're on Tarvos now, so they all look like me. No one will harm you here." And then I realize another problem needs immediate attention. I lift my chin and bark out an order. "This human needs a Hyrrokin translation chip. Immediately."

A staff member hurries to ready the dispenser.

"Wh…what's happening?"

I place both of my claws upon her shoulders. She meets my gaze again. "Have you ever had a translation chip administered?" I ask, using her human speak.

"No…" She glances with trepidation at the powerful Hyrrokin female who is fast approaching with the tool.

I pinch her chin with my claws and turn her face back towards mine. "Do not worry." I gently rub her soft skin with my thumb. "This female is going to place the language dispenser at the base of your skull and administer a tiny chip under your skin. It is painless. It will send signals to your brain, making it possible for you to read and speak the Hyrrokin language. Right now, the only reason we've been able to communicate is because I was given a chip just like this, before I left for your planet, which allows me to understand human speak. But now that we are on my planet, none of the rest of the Hyrrokin here will understand you because your language is not common. You need to have the Hyrrokin language chip implanted before you leave here if you are to communicate with other Hyrrokin on Tarvos."

She looks me right in the eyes. "I understand."

I drop my hand. "Are you ready?"

"Yes, I'm ready. Go ahead."

I motion for the employee to approach and do her job. In a moment the chip is administered, and we are done.

I switch then to my own language, to test Charlotte's readiness, "Are you ready to leave and go with me to my domicile?"

"Yes," she answers in perfect Hyrrokin, with a pleasant accent. "Yes, I'm ready and I understand you perfectly." She claps her hands with excitement. "Oh my gosh, I can speak your language now. How cool." Charlotte flashes a smile at the female who gave her the chip. "And that really didn't hurt at all. Thank you."

I keep her hand in mine as we exit the room and walk together down the hall to the lift. We step inside and I program it to take us to the roof.

"Why are we going up? Shouldn't we be going to the ground floor so we can leave?"

"We go up because my hovercraft is parked on the roof."

Her jaw drops open. "Hovercraft?"

A smile tugs at the corner of my lips. The lift stops and the door slides open. I take her hand again and we step out onto the roof and approach the hovercraft. Her human hair and the odd white skirt float in the breeze from the powered-up wind currents. My pilot warmly greets us both. The ramp lowers and I guide Charlotte in first, then I settle into the back seat next to her.

She points at the Ashmoor coat of arms that are burnished into the back of each seat. "You didn't rent this ship? This is your *personal* hovercraft?"

My lips twitch. "Let me guess, you've never been on a hovercraft before either?"

"No, of course not. Why would I?"

I take her hand again and place our joined fingers on my thigh. The hovercraft lifts gently from the rooftop.

Pure joy lights across Charlotte's features as we take flight. She gazes out the windows in stunned silence.

I smile at her indulgently. "Why weren't you as afraid of me as

HIS HUMAN WARD

the other humans were?" I ask. "You didn't run from me and scream as all the other humans on your planet did."

She looks back at me and shrugs. "I was aware that Hyrrokin existed because of my grandfather. I'd been given pictures of him, and I've already researched your species, so when you arrived I knew right away what you were. I suspect the others had never heard of your species and…and they thought…"

"They think I look like the stuff of nightmares?" I chuckle. "I've heard of this before that for some reason other species think Hyrrokin look 'scary.' This is fine, we use it to our advantage during war time." And then I think of something else. "But you looked scared and uncomfortable when you met the other Hyrrokin staff in the transporter room."

"Oh, well, they did look scary to me at first…"

"But I didn't?"

She blinks, obviously not having made this connection either. "No," she admits, "I guess I'm not afraid of *you*."

I smile again and pick up my tablet and message Barnabas, letting him know we will be landing soon.

Charlotte remains attentive to the panoramic view out the window as the hovercraft rushes over and across the main city of my home planet. The glittering skyscrapers under the sparkle of our two suns is truly stunning. She giggles with joy as we pass important landmarks and dart over two smoking volcanoes. I'm pleased to be experiencing something so mundane through her eyes.

I cannot pleasure mate with this female. I cannot. She's my ward.

And then the hovercraft lingers as it settles over my estate and begins to land on my private pad, next to Ashmoor Manor. I am eager to show her the inner workings of the manor where the Ashmoors have lived for millennia. She is after all technically now an Ashmoor. This is her lineage too.

Her jaw drops open again and she gives me an accusing

glance. "I thought you said you weren't royalty, but this looks like a palace."

"I'm not royalty. This is my home and it is called a manor. I am the thirteenth Fire Lord of Ashmoor," I remind her. I decide to not yet give her my full title or any of my secondary or honorary titles, "fire lord" is enough for now. "I'm only twenty-fifth in line to the Fire throne of Tarvos, so I'm Hyrrokin nobility, not royalty. But that is mainly an honorary title nowadays. The queen is no longer the political head of the planet, but she is still the heart and soul of Tarvos and the center of society. And she is extremely wealthy. Her generational wealth is now second only to the recent tech and finance Billionaires."

"You live here alone?"

"I am the only Ashmoor who has been here full-time for the last two years. But much of the staff lives here too, so I'm technically not living alone."

"Oh no, have I been addressing you wrong? Should I call you Lord Ashmoor?"

Etiquette decrees that I should have her call me by my title, but I find I do not want that. "No, you may continue to call me Thayne." Suddenly I imagine us both in my bed, with her calling out my first name as I bring her to completion.

I cannot pleasure mate with my underage ward. *But in one week she will be legal*, my inner devil remarks.

"You have employees that live here? The pilot of this hovercraft is also your employee?"

"Yes." I smile. "And you will meet the rest of the staff when we arrive."

The hovercraft comes to a complete stop on the landing pad and Jinos opens the door. The ramp lowers and I step out first and again take the female's small hand in mine and help her out as she rearranges layers of fabric. Strange foot coverings are on her tiny feet, the type that all humans wear. How does she walk so expertly on those pointy-tipped coverings? It is a mystery.

I guide her with me along the front terrace of the east wing.

As we walk hand-in-hand, she stares to our left at the broad expanse of formal gardens. "It's so beautiful," she breathes.

"It is," I agree absently. My eyes remain fixed at what is awaiting us at the front steps to the manor. Barnabas has assembled the staff. They are all arranged on either side of the many steps leading up to the main entrance, ready to formally greet the new member of the Ashmoor family. I am pleased and yet strangely nervous, as if this is a momentous occasion.

There's a buzz of voices. Horns turn and tilt toward each other as the staff confirm amongst themselves that I am not bringing a child to live here as originally thought, but instead I've brought a fully grown female dressed in a manner I'm certain is strange for them to witness. But as I approach, they take this change in stride and maintain their professional demeanor. My staff cares as much for this manor as I do. Most of them are experts in Ashmoor ancestry and are from families who have worked at this manor for hundreds of years. They've pledged their fealty to the Ashmoors in the ways of old. Caring for the manor as well as maintaining traditions are important to these Hyrrokin. Sometimes I find the formality tedious, but I also clearly understand the importance of carrying on the history of this esteemed line. I am this generation's caretaker of the Ashmoors and I take my responsibility seriously.

Charlotte and I stop at the base of the grand steps that lead up to the main doors of the front entrance. All the Hyrrokin in my employ at the estate are assembled above in their formal Ashmoor livery, according to their rank and seniority, including the recently arrived seasonal interns.

"Oh," Charlotte breathes. "What is this?"

I squeeze her hand and pull her forward with me. "You are about to meet everyone," I explain.

My staff stands at attention, perfectly quiet, the only sound the distant thump of the workers at the reflective pool. All one hundred Hyrrokin staff members have their eyes on me and my new ward.

I continue to hold Charlotte's hand. I raise my voice so all can hear my pronouncement. "I present to you this human, Charlotte Cruz Ashmoor, the adoptive granddaughter of the former Fire-Baron, Targek Ashmoor the fifth. This female is now legally my ward, and I am her guardian. Charlotte is nineteen years old and will turn twenty in one week. She will be living here under our care for the next full planetary rotation until she reaches the age of twenty-one. We will train her in all things Ashmoor so that when she leaves our company and comes into her inheritance, she will be proficient in the continuance of our Hyrrokin traditions." I step back and wave a hand, motioning for her to step forward and begin greeting my employees. "Lady Ashmoor, may I present to you the staff and caretakers of Ashmoor manor. Please greet them each, one at a time, so that they may present to you their titles."

She looks up at me with a sudden flash of fear in her expressive human eyes. Is my human too fragile for this? Is she not ready? I step forward, ready to assist her and join in her procession.

She holds up a palm. "No, I can do this," she whispers.

Pride warms in my chest as she swallows her nervousness and lets go of my hand. Then she lifts her chin and leaves me behind. Charlotte boldly steps forward to solely greet the Hyrrokin, as is customary.

At the bottom step, in first position, is my butler, Barnabas. I watch as he gives my ward a formal bow, offers her his name and title, and they both share a light handshake. Charlotte smiles back at him and lets him know in our Hyrrokin language that she's happy to be here and pleased to meet him, then she moves up the next step to similarly greet the housekeeper, hearing her title and name, smiling in greeting and offering her own delicate hand to the staff member. Then she steps up to meet the head chef in the same way, then she steps up and greets the head gardener and on and on she goes up the steps, stopping to shake red hands tipped with silver claws and smiling at each staff member with genuine grace.

She shows no lingering signs of the fear of Hyrrokin features that overcame her in the transporter room. Her white dress is so long it trails down a few steps behind her as she moves up the procession. The white of her dress and the absence of pigment in her skin and lack of black horns or tail is a stark contrast to the larger, red-skinned Hyrrokin surrounding her. She is easy to pinpoint as she makes her way up, step by step.

When she reaches the top, she perfectly understands the need to step across and continue. She executes two right turns to start back down on the other side, smiling wide, shaking more hands, bunching the front of her dress in her left hand as she moves down gracefully on those pointy foot coverings, step by step. I watch as she leaves no one out, making sure to also give warm greetings and handshakes at the bottom for the two young wide-eyed interns. She eventually reaches the end of introductions and steps forward to meet up with me again at the base of the steps. By now her cheeks are glowing and her eyes sparkle.

I suddenly wish my mother was here to meet this human female.

My mind flashes to my former bound, who performed this exact same task when she first arrived at the manor after we'd left the courthouse. My mother needed to accompany her up the steps, helping her with the greetings with constant prompts. Letecia stopped halfway through, claiming exhaustion, leaving fifty percent of the staff without their formal greeting. This proved to be a harbinger of her poor treatment and lack of unity with the caretakers of my line.

I take Charlotte's hand and smile wide as we perform the last leg of our journey. We both march together back up the middle of the steps, hand in hand, in between the two lines of staff on either side of us. She grasps a handful of the white fabric as we climb the steps. The assembled Hyrrokin clap and whistle for us as we pass, cheering for our new arrival.

Heh. They did not cheer for Letecia.

A porter holds the front door open for us and we step inside the grand foyer. The door closes behind us with a heavy thud and quiet returns to the manor. Grimwall and Barnabas have joined us. Now it is only the four of us—the head housekeeper, the butler and my ward and I. Charlotte lets go of my hand, taking in the grandeur of the entrance. The soaring ceilings, the grand staircase and the enormous rooms with arched windows. She turns around in circles, making sure she can see everything.

I should be happy. This female showed all the staff proper respect, and she is enchanted at the sight of the manor. Ashmoor manor is who I am, and I should be pleased that she likes the estate that is my whole world. But my former joy at the proximity of the female I want to pleasure mate morphs into dread. The portraits of my ancestors judge me, and I'm reminded of the millennia of duty and obligations that weigh heavily upon my shoulders. I take in the curve of her lips and the swell of her teats at the top of that dress. I'm too enthralled with her. This is not right.

I cannot have her. One night of pleasure mating would never be enough. Not only is she too young, and human, but I've vowed to never take another bound or start a new family.

"Lady Ashmoor, would you like me to show you to your room so you can rest and change?" Grimwall the housekeeper asks the female.

Charlotte looks to me for confirmation and I nod. It would be good for her to get settled and have time alone.

Grimwall starts up the stairs. Charlotte reaches out, ready to take my hand again and follow Grimwall, but this time I step past her and march up the stairs alone. A look of hurt flashes on her face and I feel like an ass. But Charlotte quietly follows along with Barnabas. I miss her touch, but now that we are inside the manor I am reminded of my oaths, my Ashmoor honor and my legal obligations toward this female. And most importantly I am reminded of how it went with my former bound. All seemed well too with Letecia, at first.

Then it all went to hell.

At the top of the stairs I turn and follow the housekeeper down the hall. The four of us move down one hallway, then another and finally arrive at the bedroom the staff has prepared for Charlotte, which I remember at the last minute is the nursery. We all thought I was bringing back a child. In fact, this room is next door to the room my son once used when he was alive. I haven't been in this exact hallway in over two years. I normally walk around it and access my own suite through another set of back stairs.

My palms sweat as I glance at my son's former bedroom. I haven't stepped inside his room in almost three years. Is it still the same? I declared it sealed after his death. Are all his toys still there?

Grimwall opens the door to the room that was readied for Charlotte, which is next door to Wylik's former room. I step inside and see it is decorated in purple for a small child. This will not do. Charlotte looks around, a wide smile on her face. She thinks the room is perfect, but I know it's entirely inappropriate. I cannot visit her here, and I do not want this area in use.

"Barnabas?" I growl and motion for my butler to follow me out into the hall so we can speak in private.

"Yes, sire?"

"This room will not do. I thought I was arriving with a child, but as you can see, my ward is only one week from legal adulthood. Cancel the nanny and the tutor."

"As you wish."

"I need you to place this female in the bound's suite, next to mine. I want her close while she gets used to this new world and the workings of the mansion."

His face remains entirely impassive at my outrageous request. "Yes."

"She needs all new clothing. I want a personal stylist here tomorrow with choices for her to try."

"Yes."

"Assign staff to her and make sure she's comfortable. And…" I turn back to look at Charlotte. She's standing in the doorway, watching me talk, and the way she's framed—she looks perfect. Except for that human mating dress. I hate it. "Make sure that white fabric she's wearing is eventually incinerated," I growl.

Barnabas nods and makes a note on his tablet.

"Thayne? Are you okay?" Charlotte asks with genuine concern. "What's wrong?"

She stares at me intently. It kills me that she looks truly worried for me. But how can she be worried? We just met. I glance over again at the door to my son's room, which brings up memories I'm not ready to unpack and revisit. Smoke wafts from my nostrils. "I have to leave for a meeting," I lie. "Barnabas and Grimwall will make sure you have everything you need."

Her gaze fills with sadness and she moves closer. "You… you're leaving?"

I take a step back. I've been by her side every moment since we met, but I cannot have her, and she needs to know that now. I am the fire lord and the head of the Ashmoors. Dishonor with an underage ward is unacceptable. And even if she were of age, I can never be more to her than a temporary pleasure mate, and she is too young to accept anything less than a male who can give her everything.

I am her guardian and I will protect her, even from me.

I clench my claws, trying to refrain was inhaling Charlotte's luscious scent. "You are nineteen and in my care," I remind her of the legality of our relationship. "I am your guardian and you are my ward."

She again gazes at me with eyes filled with nothing but genuine care and concern.

I turn and walk away.

My former bound seemed caring at first too. Letecia wasn't perfect with the staff, but she was kind to my mother and attentive to my every need. She loved the manor and attended all of the public gatherings. I'd been ready to give her all my heart if she'd wanted it. I let my guard down and paid the ultimate price.

I won't let it happen again.

5

CHARLOTTE

Thayne leaves, with Barnabas trailing behind and I'm left alone with Grimwall, the housekeeper.

I watch the undulation of Thayne's muscular back and the jab of his tail as he heads down the hall and then pounds his way downstairs, not once looking back at me. Jeez, he's so muscular. Muscles upon muscles. That red chest is a work art.

Huh. I purse my lips and glance around. He basically ran away from me.

Thayne became troubled the moment we walked inside the manor and the doors closed behind us. He became more upset when we got upstairs. The friendly, touchy-feely version of Thayne was replaced by a stiff and remote male with clenched fists and rapid breaths. He didn't seem angry, but instead troubled. The moment we arrived upstairs and stood in front of the bedroom he looked distressed and I wanted to help him, but he wouldn't tell me what was wrong and pulled away.

I miss Thayne already. He's my partner-in-crime. The male who took me from a bad situation and brought me to this safe place, where my future is wide open and the meanness of the past already behind me. I'm able to start a whole new chapter of my life here that includes learning of the heritage left to me by Targek Ashmoor.

My mother was unstable and she'd hated my grandfather's appearance and let it drive a wedge between her and her own mother and allowed me to be cut off from my family. But my grandmother had loved Targek Ashmoor very much. And despite the way my mother treated him, that male had still found ways to send currency to make my life comfortable and to give me opportunities. I really think my grandparents had planned that when I was of legal age according to Hyrrokin law, and therefore fully apart from my mother's influence, that they would reintroduce themselves to me. Maybe we would have had a family reunion for my twentieth birthday? We were so close to being able to start over and build a new relationship. And then it was all taken away. My mother suddenly died and then so did both of my grandparents, all three of them, months apart from each other. And now I'm alone. But I owe it to both of my grandparents to take this opportunity to learn more about the Hyrrokin species and the Ashmoors in general.

I turn back to the housekeeper, and she smiles at me, which makes her gruesome features a tad less scary. I nibble on my lower lip and decide that Thayne was probably stressed because he really did have business to attend to and I need to move on and tackle this new life and not back down. He did insist that I have that translator chip, which has certainly come in handy, and he made sure I was able to introduce myself and be welcomed by everyone in the manor… He's not leaving me high and dry. He set me up for success and he's basically telling me to take it from here.

I blow out a breath.

Okay, I can do this. I had bad luck making true friends with my roommate and her family, but that's not everyone. If Thayne and Targek Ashmoor are any indication of how the Hyrrokin conduct themselves, then I need to give this a chance. I've never been one to judge a being by their appearance alone, so actually it's been easy for me to look past the nightmare features of all these Hyrrokin and remember that inside, humans and Hyrrokin are not that different. I've learned that already from the short time I spent alone with Thayne.

I'd unfortunately never met my grandfather prior to his death, so when Thayne appeared he was the first Hyrrokin I'd met in real life. I knew of Hyrrokin only through the minimal research I'd done on the species. Then I met his pilot, who was scary, then the staff at the station. And then—gulp—I was introduced to every single Hyrrokin who works in this enormous mansion, including the grounds and outbuildings. And by now, I feel a little desensitized. They are all so much bigger than me. And the black horns on their heads and the tails make them seem even larger. Sometimes I can see smoke wafting from their nostrils.

Grimwall continues to smile, exposing sharps fangs. She guides me down the hall and I follow along. "I'm sorry about that small bedroom," she tells me, "Lord Ashmoor is absolutely right; it was not appropriate for you. We originally thought a young child was arriving at the manor so we prepared the nursery. I will show you to your new room."

Grimwall's not much taller than me and she carries a necklace around her neck with a collection of antique keys. All the females I've met so far on Tarvos wear the same type of bright shirts that cover their torso but leave their arms and neck completely bare. There aren't even any straps. Her shirt is dark pink and she wears a matching pink skirt that ends at her ankles. All the Hyrrokin are barefoot, and there is a slit at the back of her skirt which allows her tail the freedom to jab the air behind her. She looks feminine, yet no-nonsense and ready for work. I like it.

I nod in agreement and quietly follow Grimwall down a very long hallway with a window at the end. We take two different left turns and down another hallway and then we stop at another door. She takes a key from the chain at her neck and bends down to open the tall, ornate door. I take a step back to give her clearance, wanting to avoid the sweep of her pointy black tail.

"I'm not used to so many old-fashioned doors with antique locks," I tell her. "New Earth was recently rebuilt after the war, so everything there is so new..." Then the door creaks open and I gasp with delight. An exquisite room is displayed in front of me. I place a palm against my chest and walk hesitantly inside, staring in amazement at everything at once, overcome with joy at the beauty that surrounds me. I knew this place was a "palace," but seeing this room seals the deal.

The nursery I was first shown was amazing and to be truthful I didn't even know it was considered a nursery until they said it was decorated for a child. I couldn't tell that it was a children's room, and I was ready to stay there, thinking that room was nicer than anywhere I'd ever lived my entire life. But now I see the difference between the two. The last room had a small, narrow bed that was just my size, so I didn't notice it was built for a child, but in here there is a four-poster bed big enough for five people. The ceiling is high and ornate with panels and carvings. A series of tall windows frame an extended view of the front formal gardens of Ashmoor. The room is so large there is a expansive sitting area with four comfy cream-colored chairs with green pillows and a small table placed in front of the windows.

My heels click across the stone floors and dig into the thick area rugs as I speed-walk over to the windows because I have to see the view first. The view from the nursery was of the back gardens, but this room has a view of the sweeping vista leading up to the front of the mansion. I stop right at the frame of an open window and stand there for a moment, watching a distant team of Hyrrokin fill water into some sort of pond in the middle of the gardens.

Then I turn and look around again at the room and squeak with delight at the bed. The wood is ebony and the bedding is a light green. I walk over and place a hand on the gorgeous bedspread and wonder at how soft it is with such an intricate weave. There's an enormous stone fireplace on the opposite wall from the foot of the bed, and on the walls are large oil paintings of landscapes and Hyrrokin from prior centuries posed in formal clothing, similar to what I'd seen downstairs and in the hallways.

"Is this room acceptable?" the housekeeper asks.

"Of course," I sputter. "It's fantastical. I've never seen a room more beautiful in my entire life. Thank you for bringing me here."

She beams, pleased at my remark. "I'm happy you enjoy it. This was once the Dowager Ashmoor's suite."

I stop in my examination of the bedside tables and stare at her with confusion. "What is a 'dowager'?"

"Oh, a dowager is the title of the widow and mother of a member of the aristocracy. Our dowager was Lord Ashmoor's mother and she lived with him here at Ashmoor Manor, prior to her death two years ago. She didn't sleep in this actual room anymore, not since the days she was bound to the former fire lord. But this was once her room when she was the Lady of the Manor and when her bound, Torman Ashmoor, Lord Ashmoor's father was the twelfth fire lord."

"Oh." I glance around because now I'm confused. Is she saying this is technically the room for the wife of the fire lord? But I'm not Thayne's wife, I'm his ward. Why would they put me here?

"We aired it out for you because no one has used this room in fifteen years. This is why the windows are still open. But it is still maintained because we always want to be ready if it is needed, as it is now. You can use the console on the bedside table to call us for anything you might need. There is a cleaning bot assigned to this room, but you also have a personal maid named Milli."

"I do?"

"Of course. Now let me show you the rest of the suite. I'm certain you want me out of here so you can rest and relax."

I smile because she's got a point. Resting and relaxing does sound lovely, especially after the crazy day I just had.

Grimwall takes me through to the restroom and shows me how to turn on the fancy equipment. Every surface looks like it is either carved from white stone or crafted from brushed metal. The cleansing unit is big enough for a team of Hyrrokin and I can see that it has extra settings I've never used before. This manor looks old, but it is well-maintained and updated with all the modern conveniences. We pass by a very large bathtub and continue down a short hallway into the dressing room. The lights flick on to reveal an enormous walk-in closet of gleaming dark cabinets that are entirely empty.

"I was informed that you left your home planet, unable to bring any of your own clothes with you. And because we unfortunately thought a child was arriving, we do not yet have any extra clothing ready for you," Grimwall explains and points at a white robe hanging on a peg. "But you can put the robe on while you wait for new clothes to arrive, if you'd like to get out of that…um…" She sweeps her hand up and down at what I'm wearing.

I look down at the tight dress and the huge train, suddenly wishing I *could* get out of it. I'm still standing in the bridal gown and high heels I wore at the altar. It's not what I would ever choose for myself, but it is very pretty. But it's also extremely uncomfortable. And the shoes are killing me. I immediately start to kick them off. "It's a wedding dress," I explain as I bend down and slip off a shiny white heel. "Lord Ashmoor saved me from having to marry a very bad human male. I'm grateful. But you're right, I would love to get out of this dress because it's restricting and uncomfortable. I would love to relax in a robe." I stand up and look down at the stiff fabric covering my stomach and instantly realize I'll need help with the corset. "But um, before you leave, could you please unfasten the back for me?"

"Of course."

I turn around and Grimwall expertly undoes the back, the only part I can't do myself. It loosens and I hold the front up to cover myself and take in a grateful breath.

Grimwall chuckles at my obvious delight at being unfastened and free to breathe. "I will send up a tray of refreshments," she says. "Milli will arrive soon to attend to you." And then she steps out. I hear the distant click of the door to my suite.

I look around at the glamorous closet and giggle.

When I woke up this morning this was not at all how I thought my day would progress. I can't believe so much happened in one day. I was about to marry Jaden, then I found out he'd been cheating on me and he and his sister and mom actually all hated me and they were only pretending to like me so Jaden could marry me and get half of my currency.

Thayne stormed the chapel and carried me away from the altar, making it so very easy for me to get out of that wedding that wasn't going to happen. I inherited a fortune and title from my adoptive grandfather, but he'd also designated Thayne Ashmoor as my guardian in the event of his death, and now I'm Thayne's ward. I have a feeling that if I wanted, I could legally contest this whole thing. I'm a human and a citizen of New Earth. But I'm ninety-nine percent certain that if I contested the guardianship, I'd have to give up the inheritance and the title. Do I want to get away from Tarvos that bad? No. I can live here for a year and learn about all things Hyrrokin. It sounds like a fair trade-off.

I wiggle out of the dress that I never wanted in the first place. Maya had picked it out for me. Tears prick at my eyes as I remember again the person who I thought was my friend but wasn't at all. Maya's betrayal hurts more than that of Jaden or her mom. We were roommates. I'd basically only dated and then agreed to marry her brother because he was *her brother*.

I push the skirt down and step out of it, trying to forget the pain Maya caused. I cried over the betrayal for many hours last night. I'm not going to let her cause me to spend a second day crying. The three of them are probably pissed that I got away and they let my money slip through their fingers. Other than that, those three could give a shit about me.

Grr.

This beautiful dress brings up bad memories of falsehoods and broken promises. I want to leave it all behind.

Finally, my dress, underwear and accessories are all in a big, fluffy pile on the floor of the middle of the dressing room and I'm naked and exposed. I glance over at a long, full-length mirror propped against the wall. Normally, I avoid looking at myself naked because I've been trained to think my rolls, cellulite and poochy stomach are ugly. But for once I don't rush to cover myself. I step over and examine myself and…I'm not upset at what I see.

My mind flashes to all the appreciative, scorching hot looks and the intimate touches Thayne gave me the entire time we were together.

I'm not a virgin. I've dated before and had two different, short-term boyfriends. But…I've never really had anyone look at me the way Thayne did today. I place a hand on my hip and straighten my back. Then I turn around and look over my shoulder at my bare ass. I turn back to the front again and look down at myself. And for once I see my good qualities. My boobs are big, but they've got good shape. My hair is thin but at least it's shiny with natural highlights. And I've got a bright smile and nice teeth. My hazel eyes sparkle with hints of green. I like how my legs look; I think they're shapely. My skin is smooth and glows a light golden color. I rarely need makeup because my skin is so clear.

Hmm.

I grab the robe and throw it over my arm and pad barefoot through the short hallway that connects the dressing area to the bathroom. The temperature of this jungle planet is so perfect, I don't feel cold even though I know the windows are open in the front room. I reenter the bathroom and sigh with delight. This area alone is easily as large as my last apartment.

The heavy wedding makeup needs gone, as well as the way they styled my hair. I want to be fresh and clean. I'd already taken off my engagement ring and we'd never placed the wedding band on my finger. I'm one hundred percent certain that Jaden, Maya or their mom dropped to the floor to retrieve that expensive ring the moment I left.

I turn on the cleansing unit and drape the robe over a padded chair. Then I step inside the nicest unit I've ever had the pleasure to experience. Wow. The water rains down from above and is instantly warm. There isn't even a timer or a water reclamation system. New Earth is semi-arid, so this heavy spray of water is completely bizzarro to me.

Green vegetation and bodies of water are everywhere on this planet. The gardens in front of the Ashmoor estate are filled with a wild profusion of exotic flowers. I'm obsessed with xeno-botany and horticulture, so I know I'm going to love studying the plants, flowers and trees on Tarvos in comparison to New Earth. This might be my secret reason for why I'm so quickly agreeing to stay here.

The cleansing unit is amazing, and I stay inside a long time because I cannot believe how lovely and decadent it feels to use all the water I could ever want. At the end of the program my skin is cleansed and polished and my hair blown out shiny and sleek. I step out of the unit, feeling like a trillion chips of currency. No wonder there aren't any towels in this restroom—I don't need any. I'm perfectly dry when I slip on the super-soft white robe and tighten the belt at my waist.

Then I hear a knock on the door to the suite.

6

CHARLOTTE

I assume it's Grimwall with those "refreshments."
Back home on New Earth, everything is newly built, so the doors are modern sliding doors with digital alerts. I love how here at the manor all the doors require the use of actual doorknobs. The old-fashioned sound of a hand knocking against heavy wood in order to alert me to open a door is so very charming.

I step out into the main suite and turn the ornate handle of the heavy door at the entrance to the suite and creak it open. A familiar-looking, gruesome Hyrrokin female stands at attention, dressed in the same pink uniform all the female household staff wear, except hers is shorter and ends at her knees. She holds a tray of food and manages a slight curtsy while keeping everything perfectly level. "Good afternoon Lady Ashmoor. I am Milli, your personal maid. May I enter?"

Her tongue is long and forked. Are her fangs sharper than usual?

"Oh, of course," I answer, trying to keep the tremble out of my voice. My fear has returned for a moment, and I do my best to tamp it down. It's so, so strange to hear these beings, who outwardly look like they are going to attack me and bite my head off politely referring to me as "Lady." I feel like a girl on one of those fantasy vid channels. How can this be my life?

I move back to give her space because I don't want to get accidentally smacked by her shiny black tail. The female breezes past and the scrumptious scent of whatever she's carrying causes my stomach to gurgle with hunger.

"We met earlier," she reminds me over her shoulder with a cheerful tone, "but since you met so many Hyrrokin at once, I'm certain you don't remember. But again, my name is Milli. Oh, where would you like me to set this down for you?"

I look up at her, trying to hide the fact that I was examining her bare feet and deadly toenails. And I point at the table and chairs in front of the picturesque view. She nods and walks over to place the tray down for me. Then she takes a moment to explain how to operate the warm pot of Traq and how to access the sweetener and creamer that are nestled in perfect little containers. She shows me the tiny colorful plate of hot meat bites. "Take a seat and relax," she says. "Grimwall said to let you know not to worry about your lack of clothes. Your stylist will arrive first thing in the morning and will make sure you have all the clothing you need."

I sit down heavily. "My stylist?" Since when do I need a stylist? But…I look around at the splendor of the suite I was assigned and remind myself that things are very different now. First, I'm a human in need of proper Hyrrokin-style clothing and I have no idea what that entails. And also, there's going to be lots of pomp and circumstance at this manor, and I suppose I'll need to be dressed appropriately.

"Yes. We apologize that right now all you have is your robe, but this will be fixed soon. Is it alright if I take away the clothing you arrived in? We can use it to ascertain your size."

"Oh, sure." I'm actually not as interested in the idea of new clothes as I should be. What I really want to know are the whereabouts of Thayne Ashmoor, but I don't want to appear needy. He knows where I am and if he wants to see me all he has to do is come here.

I thank Milli profusely for the snack tray and she leaves with her arms full of my white dress, underwear and shoes. She gives instructions on how to order my dinner when I'm ready and she's out the door and I'm alone again.

I rearrange the pillows behind me in the comfy chair I've chosen in front of the open windows and pour myself Traq in a very large cup, stir in my preferred amounts of creamer and sweetener and take small bites of the delicious meat. A pleasant breeze flutters my hair and I smile.

This second-story view is amazing and so is the food, but all I can think of is Thayne.

Is he resentful that he's burdened with a human female he thought at first was a child but instead is a fully grown female who, according to Hyrrokin law, isn't technically an adult? It must be hard for a rich, noble guy like Thayne to suddenly learn he's responsible for some stranger who isn't even his own species. He could've said, "fuck it," and hired a team of lawyers to contest the will and never bothered to come and get me. I chuckle as I sip my Traq, remembering again how Thayne thought I was a child and instead he finds me at the altar about to get married.

What were the chances of that?

When he stomped into that church, he set off a chain of events that freed me from a doomed marriage and I'm forever grateful. I hate confrontations, so not having to tell Jaden, Maya and their mother off and just leave in such a spectacular way was much better in my mind. Also, I believe it's good that I'm here. What he said to the staff was right—I'm here to learn the ins and outs of the Ashmoors. If I'm to inherit Targek Ashmoor's currency and his title, it's only right that I understand the culture and the history I've inherited.

I finish my cup of Traq and devour all the meat bites and decide that lying down sounds like a great idea. The gorgeous four-poster bed beckons for my attention. I move a footstool over so I can step up onto the top. Then I lie down and discover it's heaven. The pillows are pliable and yet firm, as is the mattress. The green bedding is silky soft. And all I have to do is turn on my left side and I can gaze out at the panoramic view while in bed. How lovely is that?

I twirl my hair in my fingers, daydreaming about the idea of Thayne at the altar with me, as my real groom, and the two of us taking our vows and becoming husband and wife. And when he carries me away, it's to our honeymoon.

And then I curl up in my soft robe and fall asleep.

LATER I AWAKE to the two suns setting. Jeez, how long did I sleep? I stretch and lie there awhile, gazing at the details in the room, trying to fully wrap my brain around everything that happened. I can't get over the fact that I woke up this morning in Singapore, on New Earth, thinking I was getting married. Now I'm on an entirely different planet on the other side of the four sectors. Modern technology is pretty amazing.

I reach over and use the console on the bedside and speak to Grimwall. We go over the chef's menu for the evening and I try my best to pick what foods I think might be my favorite. Then I go into the restroom and use a tall, high-tech toilet and wash my hands. I do wish I had some human things with me, like socks or slippers because my feet are cold on the stone floors now that the suns are setting.

Milli soon arrives with another tray of mouth-watering food and places dinner out for me again on the table in front of the window—this time with a gorgeous view of two suns setting over the gardens.

There's also a Hyrrokin male staff member in the room, who I know I met earlier, but I'm embarrassed to admit I can't remember his name. He sets down a basket of heavy print books next to my chair and introduces himself. "I am Sylik, first assistant to the butler, Barnabas. He ordered these books brought to you and said they were to remain in your room as your own personal resource on Ashmoor ancestry."

"Oh, thank you." I bend down to finger the heavy, hardbound books. "They're beautiful. I've never touched real print books before. I promise I'll read—" I let out a squeak because Milli opens her mouth and blasts a flame into the fireplace, lighting the ebony logs. I place a hand against my chest, trying to still my breaths. Jeez, when will I get used to the flame throwing?

Both of the Hyrrokin in the room chuckle at my reaction to something so mundane. Then Milli takes a moment to turn on all the lights for me in sconces along the walls and at my bedside tables. Then they each bid me goodnight and leave with a soft click of the closed door.

I sit down in a comfy chair by the table and look through books, eat my dinner of spicy minced meat and gaze in wonder at the suns setting in a blaze of orange, pink and purple. It is very lovely and relaxing. I feel like I really did leave New Earth to go on my honeymoon, minus the groom. Which I'm sure is much better in the end.

If I hadn't learned that Maya and her family were trying to steal from me, I'd instead be on a space liner taking a cruise of the moons of Creeka, stuck in a room with Jaden, who would probably be drunk and throwing me on the bed to... I shiver with disgust at the thought of having sex with him. And what's weird is before, I wasn't disgusted at the thought. I was reasonably attracted to him and thought it could grow into more. But now that I know what Jaden was really like, and now that I've met Thayne, I can't imagine anyone else touching me but him.

I grimace because I can't possibly have sex with my older, fire lord Hyrrokin-guardian. That's crazy talk. Yes, I've been attracted to him since the moment we met, but realistically, nothing can happen between us.

Lord Ashmoor is a whole head taller than me, his skin is deep red everywhere, he has two black horns that erupt from his forehead. Two fangs peek past his lips and he has a forked tongue. A shiny, hard-looking black tail with a barb on the tip comes out of the base of his spine. And he has huge hands and feet with silver-tipped claws.

And none of this bothers me in the least.

Yes, I'm so very attracted to my guardian.

And well, what did I think was going to be the result of all that hand-holding? Why was I letting him hold my hand and in fact encouraging it? I was hot for him since the moment we met. Even now, just thinking of Thayne and those horns on his head makes me wet between the thighs—and he's not even in the room.

How is this going to work? He considers me underage. He's a freaking fire lord and I'm...his human ward. The human he's taken in for the next year. For all I know he might be second-guessing this whole arrangement and eager to be rid of me. Maybe he was upset because the reality of me living with him set in and he had to get away and have some space. Will he be happy when I finally move out to my own domicile, or move back to New Earth?

I blow out a breath and continue thumbing through the amazing books Barnabas sent me, trying to think of something besides my unrequited lust for Thayne Ashmoor.

The books are heavy, with full color pictures and lineage charts. The heavenly scent of paper and ink wafts up and I'm entranced. Never in my life have I so much as touched a print book. I've only seen them on black market vids from the original planet, and on other historical vid shows for other species. No one creates these types of books anymore. All reading is done digitally. But of course the Ashmoors have these antique books, so I treat them carefully.

After the sun sets and I finish dinner, I make sure all the windows are shut and I close the heavy drapes and move the basket of books to a chair in front of the fireplace. An actual fire crackles on the grate—not a fake imitation fire—which is so cozy. I sit back down and put my bare feet up on a plush ottoman, the blaze keeping my toes toasty warm.

I gaze into the stone fireplace, wishing I'd had the foresight to bring along my tablet. It's tucked in with my luggage back in my apartment. It would be nice to be able to message my university friends who were at the wedding, letting them know I'm perfectly safe. They must be freaking out after seeing me carried away by a Hyrrokin who was flashing flames everywhere.

Maybe tomorrow I can ask to borrow a tablet so I can get in touch with people back home?

LATER THAT NIGHT I hear a strange noise.

I shut my book with a thud and carefully set it in the basket next to me. The fire has died down but is still crackling. I turn in my chair, trying to figure out the source of that sound. Was that a cleansing unit? I hear it again and stand up and turn around. I step closer to the wall beside the fireplace, the wall that adjoins Thayne's bedroom to mine and place my ear against the wall. This time I hear a thump and possibly the stomp of feet.

Oh wow.

My pulse quickens.

He's here; Thayne is in his room next door. This whole time he's been gone but now he's returned for the night. And that's when I notice my right hand is touching a tapestry covering a slight bump in the wall. What is this? I look up and see that the fabric is hooked above to a pole and I'm able to grasp it like a curtain and move aside the entire tapestry, which exposes a doorknob. I step back and examine the whole area. There's a connecting door between our two rooms? Well, I guess this makes sense if this is the room where the fire lord's wife would normally stay. I guess they would need an easier way to see each other.

I can't stop myself; I reach out and gently try the knob, checking to see if it's locked or unlocked. And to my surprise it starts to turn, as if I could open it. I gasp and jerk my hand back. This is terrible. I can't just walk into Thayne's room like I own the place. Why oh why did he place me so close? I'm in the room right next to the fire lord. This is the room where his wife, the lady of the manor, should reside. Why am I here and not in guest quarters on the other side of the mansion?

The door suddenly opens, and I let out a squeak of surprise. I step back and pull the robe tighter around me because I'm naked underneath. Then I lift my chin and stare up at the imposing Fire Lord of Ashmoor Manor. His sash is off his chest now and he's wearing soft black pajama pants that end at the tops of his bare red feet. This allows me to fully scrutinize acres of bare chest and perfect abs. His nipples are black against his red skin. He's a study in black, red and silver.

"S...sorry," I stammer. "I just realized there was a connecting door here and..."

Thayne eyes me up and down and I swear it feels like a caress. I cannot believe how quickly I've grown used to his gruesome blood-red features. He looks noble, not scary. Aristocratic instead of nightmarish.

"Are you comfortable?" he asks.

"Um, yes. The staff has been wonderful. They've taken good care of me. I got out of that uncomfortable dress and then took a nap. And I ate dinner and read some books."

He nods, glances down along my robe again and then back up to my face. "Your stylist will arrive in the morning."

"I heard about that." Why are my cheeks so hot? And my

breasts so heavy? "Thank you. I promise I will pay you back for—"

"Unnecessary."

"Well, but I shouldn't…"

"You are my guest. I will care for you." And then he turns and grabs something off a tabletop and then he's back again, handing me a glass tablet. "This is also for you."

I take the brand new, fantastically expensive glass tablet in my hands, the latest model all beings wish they could afford, and stare at it with wonder. I run a finger down the sleek side. "This…is for me?" I breathe.

"Yes, I had it coded to you. This is yours so you can remain in contact with whomever you please."

"I'm just borrowing it, then I can return it when I leave and…"

His jaw clenches. "No, it is yours to keep."

"But I don't want to be a burden."

"You are not a burden. I am pleased you are here," he says with a gruff voice.

"You are?" I smile. "Oh, and how are *you* feeling? I was worried about you earlier. You looked upset and I was—"

"I am doing well, thank you for asking. Goodnight, female. Sleep well." Then he shuts the door in my face and locks it for good measure.

Oof. That was abrupt.

I bite my lip, turn back to sit again in my comfy chair and play with my brand-new tablet.

7

CHARLOTTE

The next morning I'm served breakfast in bed, and I cannot believe how these beings are spoiling me. What did I do to deserve all this luxury?

Another cheerful fire crackles in the fireplace, this time to ward off the morning chill. My dreams last night were filled with sexy images of a certain fire lord guardian who sleeps in the suite next door to mine.

As a young child living in the Singapore ghetto, I relied on natural resources to heat and cool our shack. None of us had any power beyond what could be cut down or dug up on our planet to burn. Sewer water ran down the streets and I used an outdoor toilet or a chamber pot. There was no running water, and we were lucky to have a neighborhood well. Food dispensers and clothing fabricators didn't exist. Neither did med labs. We are no longer slaves to the Hurlians and the great rebuild has changed everything for the better.

My small on-campus apartment was hermetically sealed from the elements and climate controlled and I loved it. I thought I'd hate the return of real fire and a door to physically open and other "uncivilized" relics of the humans' former oppression on a primitive hostage-planet, but…I enjoy this dichotomy of ancient and modern. I like how the Hyrrokin don't just demolish the old to make way for the new but maintain and upgrade their history to keep it livable for future generations. I'm learning that not all old things are bad. Sometimes beings rush a bit too fast toward the modern and forget how good some of the old ways were.

Later, I plan on opening the windows again to let in a fresh breeze and the scent of flowers in bloom.

"Your stylist has arrived," Milli announces.

I sit up straighter. "Oh really? Already?" Then I take a last sip of Traq, brush crumbs off my chest, and stand up from the bed, still dressed in the robe from yesterday. I'm nervous because my only prior experience with someone measuring and dressing me was with the seamstress and bridal gown designer from the wedding. And that wasn't good.

The door opens and a smiling Hyrrokin female dressed in bright yellow strides into my suite. She's carrying a few bags over her shoulders, and she walks right up to me and puts out a clawed hand for me to shake. The stylist wears the same type of sleeveless shirt they all wear, and I love the look of her black tail against the cream of her elegant slacks. The Hyrrokin are all thick and muscular, even the females. They all look so strong and powerful. Her fangs and horns aren't even bothering me. And I think her tail looks delicate and edgy. She has on sparkly earrings and a chunky gold necklace.

"Good morning, Lady Ashmoor," she says with a commanding tone. "My name is Lorki Limestone and I'm here to dress you and to also stock your wardrobe."

I return her handshake. I have a feeling Lorki Limestone is the epitome of Hyrrokin fashion and beauty. "I'm Charlotte Cruz Ashmoor," I say unnecessarily. "It's nice to meet you."

She pauses to look me up and down. "I was told you were human, but I still can't believe it."

I wince.

Lorki puts down her bags and snaps her fingers. A team of more Hyrrokin bring in racks of clothes. Suddenly the room is full of her assistants and they get right to work and rearrange the chairs in my room into a semi-circle.

Milli arrives with another tray of refreshments and gives me a wink of encouragement. I smile back at her as she walks over to strip my bedding and remake my bed, so grateful for her help. Milli radiates genuine caring, which is important to me after the hell I went through so recently on New Earth. It's going to be a long time before I trust anyone so easily again, but if I were to trust someone, it would be Milli.

"Grimwall sent me that white dress you wore yesterday," Lorki explains, "so I was able to use that to extrapolate your size. I spoke to Lord Ashmoor too and he gave me additional details about your size and what he wants you to wear."

I blink. "He did?"

"Yes," she smiles. "He let me know what types of dinners and functions you would be attending so what types of clothing you will need."

Warmth spreads across my chest at the thought of Thayne speaking of me to this female, making plans for what I'll need—hopefully to go out with him at my side. "I've never worked with a stylist," I admit, "I've only ever worn clothes from a clothing fabricator."

She waves a hand. "Oh, clothing fabricators are great for general wear. But I'm here to make sure you have clothing that matches Hyrrokin culture and high fashion. And clothing that also matches our weather. This is definitely one of the toughest assignments I've ever been given—dressing a human in clothing that is appropriate for Tarvos, but also comfortable for your species. Don't worry, I researched humans and I've learned your particular bodily needs so I think I've got everything you might need. As you can see, I've brought many options for foot coverings."

I clap with delight when I see the rack of shoes and socks.

She laughs. "Are you ready to start trying on clothes so we can decide what is going to stay and what is going to go, or needs to be fitted?"

"Oh, yes, of course."

Then they all stop and stare at me, and I wonder if they expect me to strip naked in front of them, because that's not happening. Some of her assistants are male. And also, I don't know any of these beings.

Milli clears her throat and motions to a tall trifold screen they must've just set up.

"Oh thanks," I giggle and gratefully step behind the screen and slip off my robe. And then they start handing me clothes, draping them over a nearby chair for me to grab and we start a back-and-forth assembly line.

I try on clothes, step out from the screen to show everyone the result and then there's a "group decide." Grimwall and Milly are there too, giving their opinions. There's a general claws up or down that includes my opinion, the assistants and Grimwall and Milly, but Lorki always has the final say. I just go with what they want because I don't know anything about Hyrrokin fashion, nor did I know anything about New Earth fashion, as Maya often liked to remind me.

The clothes I'm trying on are fabulous because they fit and aren't ever too tight. My wide hips didn't seem to bother Lorki. And it's not always about covering up my rolls, instead the clothes are tailored to highlight my waist, my cleavage and my legs. In fact Lorki often makes comments about how perfect she thinks my figure is and that I need to show it off. No one here thinks I'm too big to be wearing high fashion. They're just amazed at the hair on my head, my lack of a tail and the fact that I wear "shoes."

The whole thing evolves into sort of an impromptu Hyrrokin fashion show. Trying on new clothes is much more girly fun than

I ever thought it would be. The clothes are form-fitting and expose a lot more skin than I'm used to, but I start to enjoy the idea of showing off my curves instead of hiding them. Wine is brought in, glasses are poured, and everyone laughs and tells jokes and funny stories. I change clothes between sips of Hyrrokin wine. The taking off and trying on of all the clothes takes so long, we end up pausing to have lunch together in my room.

By the time the stylist and her team leave, my closet is full. They took some pieces with them that they want to tailor to fit me better, but there's still so much left that I feel like I can't possibly wear it all. The once empty closet is now bursting with clothes that are beautifully displayed according to color and size.

The drawers are lined with carefully folded panties and bras. Tube top shirts in a rainbow of colors line one whole wall. There are skirts, both short and long, and a variety of different pants. Everything is of the highest quality. And along another wall, behind lighted glass doors, is a display of gowns and evening wear, along with matching shoes. This is stuff that normally only the rich and famous wear, and it's here for me. Drawers of expensive-looking jewelry. Rows of shoes for a variety of situations. Even a soft pair of slippers I can put on immediately. The bathroom is also stocked with makeup and lotions.

Lorki made sure I have clothing for all types of situations, not just for going out and needing to look fancy or sexy. There are pajamas and loungewear too and clothes I can wear if I want to go outside and get dirty. I learned the rainy season is fast approaching, so there is lots of rain gear I will use later. She even left me boots and socks. It was comical watching her and the other Hyrrokin in the room pick up and stare quizzically at my "human foot coverings."

I bring up the subject of body hair, which none of them understand because Hyrrokin are hairless beyond their eyelashes. The cleansing unit has every setting imaginable except hair removal, so I ask for old-fashioned razors. After much discussion and research on tablets, Lorki's assistants discover how to get this sent to me.

I end up changing into a pair of white underwear, a pale blue tube top, and another white robe over that and I slip into a pair of fuzzy pink slippers. And it's so, so comfortable. This robe is fresh and new and the one I was wearing before is taken away for cleansing. I realize there isn't a washing unit for clothing anywhere in the suite, so all of my clothing will always be hand-washed by staff and returned. I cannot believe.

"Lord Ashmoor requests your presence for dinner tonight at sunset in the formal dining room," Grimwall says on her way out, like it's nothing.

"Oh wow."

"Don't worry," Lorki chirps with delight as she packs up, "I already knew about that, and I left you out an outfit to wear tonight that will be *perfect*. Don't forget that you can ping me on your tablet anytime. I am always available to consult on what you should wear to any occasion, and we can fix anything that is broken, or we can bring you new items."

I thank Lorki and her staff profusely. After lots of hugging and promises to keep in touch, they're all gone and I'm alone again. It's like they were never here, and the room suddenly seems so very quiet. The food and drinks are all gone, and everything is cleaned up. The chairs are all back in their original places where they belong. And Milli was kind enough to leave a snack tray. I sit and eat and drink with my feet up on an ottoman while I tap on my fancy new tablet. And I end up lying down on the soft bedding and taking a nap, because the bed is again just so darn comfortable.

HOURS later I wake up and see what time it is and squeak with dismay because the suns are low on the horizon. I can't believe how much good sleep I've been getting since I arrived—I don't normally ever sleep this much.

I quickly hop into the cleansing unit and wash. This time I'm also able to spend time shaving. The blowout at the end leaves my hair dry and shiny. Then I enter the dressing room and find the outfit Lorki left for me. It's impossible to miss. A beautiful pale green dress hangs on a single display rack. She left the shoes she thought I should wear tonight with the dress, along with the underwear and earrings. It's a complete outfit and I appreciate that I don't have to hunt and peck, I can just put on what she's already picked out.

I try it all on and step in front of the mirror and I love how it looks. And I can't help but wonder what Thayne will think of it. He's only seen me in the wedding dress and then a robe. But now I'm dressed like a Hyrrokin female, with the addition of foot coverings. The top is the same type of tube top they all wear, and the skirt is flowy and ends right at my knees. It's all the same color of pale green, which I realize looks good on me. I slip on the nude-colored heels and then sit down to apply the fancy makeup the stylist left behind for my human complexion. I've never been one to wear a lot of makeup, just a bit to brighten my face, but I enjoy playing with the makeup Hyrrokin females wear. I apply some blush, a smidge of mascara and some light lipstick.

Finally, I'm ready. I glance at the mechanical clock on the wall. Right on time.

I've spent a day and a half in my suite so it's good to get out. Now that I have all the appropriate clothes, I really, really want to leave my room, even if it's just to go downstairs. After all, there's a whole mansion I've yet to explore.

I open the door and look both ways down the hall. It's empty and quiet. Thayne didn't return to his room and ready here for dinner, but he could've arrived and left when I was in the cleansing unit. Or maybe he got ready elsewhere?

Too bad we couldn't have just met here and walked down together...

And suddenly jealousy hits me hard as I think of something I haven't yet: What if he's got a girlfriend on the side? A man as virile as Thayne must have pleasure mates. To humans he looks scary, but I have a feeling that amongst the Hyrrokin he's an eligible bachelor. I whimper at the thought of Thayne Ashmoor, the male I wish I had for myself, having someone else. What if I think he's single but he isn't?

I remember how he held my hand when we first met and the way he looked at me last night. I'm fairly certain he feels the same attraction for me that I do for him. But for all I know he might just be waiting for me to be "of age" so we can be temporary pleasure mates, while he keeps another girlfriend on the side. I have no idea.

Is that something I would want too? An affair with him and then I leave a year from now and hardly see him again and maybe in a few years we run into each other at a Hyrrokin function and he has a wife and kids?

My heart literally hurts at the idea. It's sad and depressing and something that would make me cry for a very long time. Obviously, I'm not a pleasure mate kinda gal, especially when it comes to Thayne Ashmoor.

For all I know, Thayne might have a bevy of pleasure mates he rotates through, and if I choose to be with him, I'd be on his list as his "Thursday night female" or something. Yuck.

I blow out a breath, trying to keep my mind off these depressing thoughts and take the same route out of this wing that I used to arrive in. I pass by the nursery—the same room they were first going to place me in—and I pause to daydream for a moment about happy half-Hyrrokin, half-human children laughing and giggling in these hallways.

When I was here yesterday for the tour of the purple room, Thayne stared very intently at the room next door to the one I ended up not using. I stop and stare at it too. What is in that room? I step up and press my ear against the door, but I can't hear anything inside. I give the door a light knock. No one answers. Then I try the old-fashioned doorknob and it's locked.

Heh. It's a mystery. I keep walking down the hall, determined to later discover what so upset Thayne about that room. I hate the idea of him being upset.

Then I find the staircase we used yesterday, and I carefully walk down the grand steps, feeling like a girl in a story in one of those ebooks I read. At the base of the stairs, I'm greeted warmly by two male porters. I let them know I'm trying to meet Lord Ashmoor for dinner and one of them puts his arm out and I take his elbow, like I've seen pictures of in the books they left me. The Hyrrokin staff member walks me down another hall and we stop at a huge set of double doors.

He opens one of the doors and I see Thayne Ashmoor, seated at the head of an enormous table, looking both scary and handsome as usual.

8

THAYNE

My ward enters the dining hall and I stare at her luscious form far too long.

This epic lust I hold for her remains at a constant low-level blaze. How will I keep my desire banked for a whole year while she lives in my domicile? It seems impossible.

I meant to stay away, but I only managed to maintain my own rule for a matter of hours and then I opened the connecting door to our suite. My excuse was the tablet. That damn tablet I could've given to her at any time or ordered Barnabas to send to her.

I'd left Charlotte to the excellent care of my staff while trying to keep busy, saying I had business to attend to, and that was only a partial lie—there is always more business. Meetings, disputes to settle and currency to manage. I own Ashmoor estate, the organic agribusiness and also the adjoining royal preserve, and a myriad of other lucrative businesses, some of which were inherited and many more which I've acquired. Ashmoor Corporation is large and varied with thousands of employees. I have many competent directors and managers, but there is no board. I am fully in charge. My word is law and I guide the Ashmoor brand with a tight fist. But I do take time off to rest, and so here I am, spending my down time with my gorgeous human ward.

Charlotte pauses in the entryway. I watch as her gaze travels, taking in the dining room my line has used for generations. I enjoy her reactions to the home I was born and raised in. Everything here is old news to me. I ate at this table as a child, with my father siting in the seat I now occupy. I have been here my entire life and now I am able to experience my world from the viewpoint of a female who is from an entirely different species. All of her reactions to Ashmoor Manor fascinate me.

My ward is no longer wearing that atrocious white fabric and now wears a dress with a top cut in the typical Hyrrokin style. The stylist has done an excellent job with Charlotte's clothing. The green fabric fits her torso nicely and leaves her arms and neck exposed to my gaze. She wears a short skirt that wraps around her wide hips and stops at her knees. Her curves are utter perfection, as if crafted to my exact specifications. I love a large ass and hers is lush. Her feet are covered with pointy-heeled foot coverings. I'll have to get used to this strange human trait. I would prefer her barefoot, as she was last night when I found her covered in nothing but her robe, but her feet do appear very soft and in need of protection.

Charlotte Cruz Ashmoor is easily the most beautiful female I've ever encountered. Her scent, the way she moves, the sway of her hips. It's all enchanting.

I do not need to eat dinner with her. I usually eat in town at the club or in my room or in my office. This dining room has remained empty for the last two years, since my mother's death. But tonight, I chose to take final meal in the formal dining hall at Ashmoor Manor with my ward because I can't stop thinking of her and this is the room where I ate every night with my family while growing up, and later with my bound when she wanted to join us, and with my mother...and son. It seems only right that my ward would be here too.

If I eat with Charlotte I can monitor her whereabouts and her progress, like a proper guardian should. Last night when I opened the connecting door to our rooms, I was again checking in on her. But it might be a mistake to have her next to me in the bound suite. I had to slam the door and lock it to refrain from touching her. She was naked underneath that robe and her bare feet were entirely too lickable.

Letecia never wanted the bound's suite. Nor had she ever suggested we sleep together, like my parents had. And strangely I hadn't protested when she left my bed after our quick sessions of sex. I'd thought she was right—that we needed our space. "Absence makes the heart grow fonder," she'd say as her reasoning for our separation. And at the time it made complete sense.

My former bound lived in the wing where normally guests would stay, on the opposite side of the manor from me, our son, and my mother. Letecia had two rooms remodeled into an enormous suite and office, combined with a small dining area. This allowed her to live without needing to meet up with me or my mother in the main common areas. She was even able to bring in guests to separately entertain. After our son was born we ended up living very divided lives. But somehow this was acceptable.

I can't imagine living this way with Charlotte. I placed her in my mother's old room, without even consulting the female. But she did not seem displeased to know she was so close. Grimwall let me know that my ward was pleased with her room and thinks it's beautiful exactly how my mother left it.

Charlotte finally steps inside and greets me as the head porter starts to seat her in the traditional position as the dowager or where my former bound sat, which is far from me, at the opposite end of the long table.

I have lived with this placement my whole life, without complaint, talking to my mother or Letecia from a distance. But today it displeases me. "No," I order. "I want her next to me." I point at the spot to my right, at my elbow.

The porter's eyes widen at this breach of etiquette, but he rushes to do my bidding.

"Oh, you don't have to—" my female begins.

I rap my claws on the ancient, gleaming ebony. "You *will* sit next to me," I declare.

Her jaw clenches because I know she hates it when I make arrogant demands. She is adorable when she's angry.

The staff sets up her place setting at the new position, which is at the corner next to mine and fills her glass with Hyrrokin wine. The porter pulls out her chair at her new seat and my ward walks the length of the table, her ample hips swaying in her sexy short dress. I watch her the entire time. She takes the seat, and he pushes her in.

I can't stop staring at her lush chest. Finally, I drag my gaze up. Her breath quickens and her cheeks heat. Her sweet arousal again permeates the air and I am pleased that this female continues to desire me. I smile, satisfied to have her so close while I partake of evening meal. I pick up my tablet and tap out a quick note to Barnabas to let him know to make sure she's always here with me at dinner.

She takes out a napkin and places it on her lap for some reason. Then she stares at the array of utensils on each side of her plate. "I don't know how to use all of these," she admits.

"Do not worry, just follow what I do. I will teach you." I am not in the least bit annoyed at her lack of knowledge, I find it fun to teach her this. It makes it all new for me again. The first course is served, and I model for her which utensil to use to spear the hot meat bites.

"I like that dress much better on you than what you wore when I first met you at that human gathering," I tell her.

She laughs. "I like it better too. This dress is much more comfortable. And I really love the clothes that Lorki picked out for me. Thank you for sending her to me. She and her team were wonderful to work with."

I swallow my food and grin back at her.

"I'll pay you back for all of this," she says.

My brow furrows. "Pay me for what?"

"That entire wardrobe and the stylist. That was too much. Lorki filled the entire closet with enough clothes for a whole year. I know you said last night you didn't want me to pay for anything, but I was thinking about it again and it seems wrong for you to support me. It must be so expensive. I'd feel better if you kept a tab of what I'm spending now while I'm your ward and then you can bill me when I gain my inheritance."

"I will do no such thing," I growl. "You are here, under my protection. I am taking care of you. I do not require any of your inheritance to care for your needs." In fact, Targek Ashmoor was my poor relation. His "fortune" is inconsequential compared to mine, or that of most of my line. The male was notorious for barely monitoring his investments and allowing their growth to stagnate. I pause to show Charlotte how to cut into her blood pudding and then add, "But one thing I will do for you is I will switch your investments over to my personal guidance. I will audit your accounts and look for ways to increase your wealth."

The room grows quiet because the staff are in awe of my generous gesture. I look up thinking the female will be pleased at this boon. Many Hyrrokin over the years have begged me to personally take over management of their investments, but I always decline.

Charlotte's lips thin. "I'd prefer if you didn't do that. I'm sure I can hire professionals to manage my currency, so you don't have to bother with my accounts."

"You do not trust me with the management of your currency?" I sputter.

She waves a bloody knife in the air. "Well, it's just that, you know, you inherited all of your wealth. I'm sorry, but I'm worried you might be used to having money handed to you, that you didn't have to work for. I'd like to take some time to hire a wealth management company, like the ones they have on Salo. Those beings do nothing but grow money."

"You think I won't do a good job with increasing your wealth?"

"Well, you do seem to have a lot of expenses…"

"You think I'm a spoiled Lord who's burning through his inheritance and doesn't know how to manage the money that was left to me?" I laugh. Barnabas has quietly entered the dining hall and I see he must've heard this exchange because he is laughing too. It's hilarious.

She glances around at the chuckling staff who now line the walls and her cheeks pinken. "Okay, I guess I can let you try…"

"She'll let me *try*…" I bang a claw on the table, laughing harder.

Now the room is full of laughter. Two porters bend over and slap each other's backs. Barnabas wipes moisture from the corner of his eyes.

She tosses her napkin down on the table. "What is going on here? Why is everyone laughing? What is so funny?"

"Charlotte…Charlotte," I try to catch my breath and explain, "there are only three beings who are wealthier than me on this planet. Aegir Touchstone, who invented the finance program that changed the way we do personal finance, and his brother, who is an investor in Aegir's business and also the lucky owner of a sub-illibrium mine. The queen is the third wealthiest citizen on Tarvos. And the fourth being is me, the Fire Lord of Ashmoor. I inherited this estate when it was on the verge of bankruptcy, and I've modernized it and raised it in value to what it is today."

"Oh wow. Congratulations. That's a huge accomplishment."

"Thank you. Now, will you trust me enough to manage your investments?"

"Yes," she agrees. "I'd love for you to manage my accounts and thank you very much for offering."

I take a large swig of ale, still smiling wide. This is the most fun I've had in ages.

The porter serves the main course, which tonight is charred wild beast. My favorite. I lean back as two flaming plates are positioned in front of each of us. The fires of each plate blast so high they almost reach the ceiling. It is a glorious display. I'll have to thank chef later for his skills in this matter.

Charlotte squeaks with dismay and scoots back from the table. I blow out her meal for her, then blow out my own. She visibly calms down after the wind dies and the fires are banked. I decide then I will always be the male who banks her flames. I show her the next two utensils to use so she can eat her charred meat. "Cut into yours with smaller bites than I do. Your lack of fangs and blunt human teeth necessitate small cuts." And then I use my long fangs to tear at a large chunk, trying to display for her how good this meat is.

She pierces a tiny chunk with her fork and takes a small, tentative human bite. She chews and swallows then a smile widens across her gorgeous face. "Ooh, it's so good. The meat is tender and tastes wonderful."

I am pleased that she likes this meal as much as I do. After we finish the wild beast, we both use the water bowls and towels on the table to wash our face and claws.

"What was it like growing up on New Earth," I ask, suddenly interested in human affairs.

Charlotte smiles up at the porter as he places a small dessert in front of her. She lifts the next utensil in her delicate fingers and answers, "It was better as I got older but was harder when I was young. I was a baby when the Hurlians were kicked off of New Earth. Just prior to that, my father was snatched by the Hurlians and never returned. So, I never got to meet my father."

"I am sorry," I say with genuine remorse, perturbed at the thought of Charlotte living for so long without her father.

"My mom took my father's disappearance really hard. They were in love, and I was so small when he was snatched. It happened right before her eyes and she couldn't save him, no one could. I think she never recovered and went into decline. She isolated us from her parents and she ended up addicted to Opidiz."

I wince because I know what a scourge this particular drug has been since it's creation in a rogue lab two decades ago. It has ruined the lives of billions of beings in the four sectors.

"I didn't grow up in the same household as my grandparents. Sadly, I didn't even know they were alive. They'd lived in the wild lands of my planet, on a very large property. I guess because Targek was Hyrrokin, they both knew how most humans would treat his appearance, so they were happier living in the country. They lived very far away from me, on the other side of the planet. I was told they'd passed away when I was little, and we didn't have any other family. My mother had a hard time keeping a job and we moved around a lot. But when I got older, I was given a stipend to live off of by a mysterious benefactor and I made sure I saved a lot of it."

I crook an eyebrow ridge. "Mysterious benefactor?"

She meets my gaze. "Yeah. I think it was my grandparents. I never knew they were helping me all along. But my life was super charmed. There was always something that happened that helped me out. I was given a scholarship to a fancy girl's boarding school in Singapore. And then I won another scholarship to a university that had recently opened on New Earth. Prior to this everyone had to leave our planet for higher education. I decided to stay and go to school on my home planet. It was free, so why not? The scholarship came with a stipend for housing, food and clothing, so I've been set. The moment I was old enough I was able to successfully move out, avoid my mom and her sketchy friends and have my own life, which was nice."

I reach out and take her small hand in mine. "I'm certain your grandparents were happy to see their currency put to good use."

"You know what worries me?"

"Hmm?"

"I worry that the reason why they kept away from me is that they thought my mother had poisoned my mind against Hyrrokin and that I'd want nothing to do with them."

"Did she do that to you?"

"No. My mother did tell stories of my step-grandfather, who she said looked like the devil. She'd hated him before he died. But that was all. She mainly kept silent, pretending they didn't exist. And when I got surprise money, I learned to keep it from her, not because I knew who it was from, but because I was worried she would take it from me and spend it on drugs."

"Your mother stole the currency meant for your food, clothing and education and spent it on drugs?"

"Yes. But that was when I was younger. I'm guessing my grandparents got smarter about it and stopped sending currency that she could take, because beings would show up and tell me I'd won a scholarship. Or that I'd won a lottery and here were new clothes. It just kept happening. All the while it was them, trying to help me."

"Did your mom know it was them?"

"I think so? But other times it was so well explained away, she got to where she just snorted about how lucky I was. And why couldn't I win things like trips on space liners or currency?"

I let go of her hand. "I'm sorry that happened to you."

"It wasn't so bad, especially after I got older and got away. The last two years were really good, living at assigned housing for university and going to school. I hadn't even seen my mother in the years prior to her death." Her lips twist. "Yes. It was sad. My mom, my grandmother and then my grandfather all died around the same time in the last few months. The worst part is that I never got to know my own grandparents. I feel cheated of that time with them."

"That *is* sad," I agree. Then I ask another question, trying to take my ward's mind off her worries. "And now that you're here...what do you think of the manor?" I ask, trying to change the subject from something that makes her heart ache to a new subject that she might enjoy. Her past was terrible, but I am here now and I will make sure her future is bright. Also, I'm truly interested to hear her reaction to the domicile that has housed my ancestors for millennia.

She perks up. "Oh, I love it here. The suite you placed me in is beautiful."

I grunt, remembering how my former bound hated the sight of that room, declaring it old and decrepit. Not even bothering to soften her words or tone for my mother's benefit.

"I like how there is the old here mixed alongside the new at Ashmoor manor."

I nod because that's what I love most about this mansion too.

She cocks her head. "You know, I can be sitting in a chair in that room, after having used a high-tech cleansing unit, and after having arrived here in a hovercraft. A cleaning bot can be moving near my feet, but then I'm sitting in front of an ancient stone fireplace that is crackling with a real fire. There are print books in my basket and oil paintings of your ancestors on the walls. And I'm brought organic food on trays by real beings. There's actual staff who do maintenance alongside the bots. I like having real beings to speak to rather than AI."

"Are you still afraid of us?" I question.

She blinks with surprise. "No. Well, maybe for a moment when Milli first arrived and then when any of you flash-flame, it's hard for me to get used to. But afraid? No."

She's never been afraid of me.

At first this could be explained away due to the fact that she'd already learned of Hyrrokin. And she already knew of Targek's goodwill and therefore thought of my species as "nice." But there still remains the fact that she knows of my high-standing position in Hyrrokin society and my wealth and yet still treats me like a friend. Which I appreciate. I assume it's because she's human and doesn't truly understand the layers of Hyrrokin formality that separate me from most citizens. But I don't think that's the real reason. I think we just get along. I enjoy spending time with this female. As Thayne and Charlotte, instead of guardian and ward.

"You seem mature for someone so young," I comment. "This might be why you are stoic in the face of what others of your age and species might abhor."

She lifts her eyes. Heh. I think she was staring at my forearms.

"I've been told that before." She shrugs. "Beings do sometimes tell me that I'm mature for my age. I think it's because I basically raised myself. I had to be on it. Someone had to make sure the bills were paid and that I was fed."

Smoke wafts from my nostrils.

She meets my dark gaze. "Oh, sorry, I didn't mean to make it sound that bad...let's not forget that I was also given lots of opportunities." She waves a hand. "I mean, look where I'm at right now. How many humans are given these kinds of experiences? I am humbled that my Hyrrokin grandfather adopted my mother when her real father died, and then, despite how terribly she treated him, he didn't blame me for her behavior and continued to keep me as his heir."

"A human has never been inside of this manor before," I tell her. "You are the first."

Her eyes dart again to my forearms. And this time I clench my fists for her enjoyment. She catches her breath.

My lips twitch.

"I'm the first human at Ashmoor Manor? Wait, is that good or bad?" She fingers her wine glass and looks at me bashfully, "I mean, how do you really feel about a human being as the heir to Targek Ashmoor and now part of your extended Ashmoor family lineage?"

I lean back in my chair and give this question the serious response it deserves. "I am surprisingly unaffected at having a strange human in my midst," I admit. "There have been humans relocating on Tarvos, so at least I've heard of your species. My neighbor recently married a human…"

Her mouth drops open. "Your neighbor married a human? When? A man or woman?"

"There is a female human living next door on the Strikestone estate. I believe she is older than you, but close in age. Her name is Ariana Strikestone. She is the bound of my neighbor, Skoll Strikestone."

"Oh, I would love to meet her."

"I'm certain you will. She was told that you are arriving. I can't imagine her staying away for long. Strikestones have a habit of showing up when an Ashmoor least expects it."

Charlotte claps her hands, which I've noticed she does when she's happy.

"What are your plans after you turn twenty-one?" I ask, wanting to learn more about this female.

"Oh, well…" She tells me of her plans to study xeno-botany at university on New Earth. I know I should tell her about my brother, but I don't. I'm not ready to share her with him. I am keeping her with me and the staff, for now.

"I don't really know what I'll do yet and where I'll live," she adds. "I just want to learn more about what I'm interested in and one day I…I'd like to be married and have a family. I guess because I don't have any family of my own."

A weight settles on my chest. I set down my tankard of ale. "Tomorrow night I have a business function to go to and I will bring you as my guest," I inform her. "It is a charity auction." I used to bring my former bound to these types of functions and parties, until she began refusing to accompany me. Later I brought along my mother, but for the last two years I've gone alone, if at all. I've already informed Charlotte's stylist of her needs as Lady Ashmoor.

"Are you sure you want me to…?"

"Yes. I'm not going to hide you away as an underage child, or an odd human who I'm ashamed is living in my manor. You will take your place proudly as my ward and a new member of the Ashmoor family. You are, after all, a fire-baroness."

She grins, exposing a dimple in her cheek. "Okay."

WE BOTH FINISH OUR DESSERTS, then Charlotte stands and leaves first for bed.

I bow, bid her goodnight and retreat to my own first-floor office, as I usually do, to continue working. This time of night, when the staff has all gone to bed, or left for their own homes, is my favorite time to get work done. Even Barnabas isn't around and is only available via emergency message.

I work at my desk, finishing communications. I take time to read through all the messages we've received from customers and retainers. I like to know what is being said about the Ashmoor organization so I can head off problems and keep a handle on future trends.

After a while, I move over and sit in a chair in front of my crackling fireplace, holding another finger of amber fire-alcohol in my claw, discontent at the lack of Charlotte's scent in my vicinity. I imagine her doing this same thing, sitting in her own room upstairs—in front of her own fire, alone. I glance over at the empty space next to me and decide I need a second chair placed next to me in this room.

In the entire three years since the death of my former bound, I haven't once met another female I wanted to pleasure mate. And I've vowed to never request another female as my bound.

And yet now I want nothing more than to walk upstairs and bring this underage female into my room, have her underneath me and afterwards hold her in my arms and lick her skin. And then fall asleep with her by my side.

My ward. What is wrong with me?

I glance at the calendar, knowing I have five more diurnals until she is legal.

I make my way upstairs and I don't see a crack of light under her door. I step into my own room, the same room I've slept in for the last fifteen years. This entire time the suite next to mine has remained empty, a relic of happy times, when my parents were mated. They slept together in this room and my mother used her own room as extra space, an extended dressing room and sitting area, with a bonus extra bed if needed. She was able to decorate it however she saw fit, without my father's say. They agreed on decorations for the bedroom they shared, but the room next door was hers alone.

After my father passed and when my mother moved to her dowager suite to allow me to take position as fire lord, she always wished my future bound would one day take the bound's room over as her own, carrying on this Ashmoor tradition. My mother was devastated that Letecia never moved in. The room my ward sleeps in has historically been the room of all the bounds of the Ashmoors.

I frown at the connecting door. Last night I locked it to keep myself from behaving inappropriately. But what if Charlotte awakes and needs me in the middle of the night?

I walk over and unlock the door.

And then I go to bed and fall asleep.

9

CHARLOTTE

I love sleeping in the dowager's suite.

Milli is already there this morning, pulling back the heavy curtains and letting in the sunlight. The room next door is quiet, and I suspect Thayne has already left for the day. When does this man sleep? Last night after dinner, I didn't hear him when he came up to his room for the night.

Is it weird that I'm trying to learn and anticipate Thayne's schedule? I think I'm still swooning from that magical dinner we shared last night. It's just…it was so wonderful eating with him in the elaborate dining hall. Like something out of a fairy tale. The table was so very long and shiny, built for huge parties. Heavy chairs lined the walls and there was a lot of space at either end of the room—the table could accommodate even more guests.

And not long after I arrived, he'd demanded, in that arrogant way of his, that I be seated right at his elbow. I didn't mind of course, because otherwise I would've been trying to shout at him from across the room. It's just that he never, ever says please or thank you to anyone.

But as soon as I was seated next to the fire lord, I forgave his arrogance because I was so close I could watch every flex of his powerful arms. I'm totally addicted to Thayne's forearms. You'd think I'd be more into his corded neck, or the dip and curve of his abs, or his hard biceps. Nope, it's those veiny forearms. I kept sneaking peeks at them last night when he wasn't looking.

I sit up and stretch, trying to remind myself in the cold daylight of morning that nothing will come from my obsession with this male. Yes, he holds my hand often, but maybe he does that with all the females he socializes with? It's nothing special. *Nothing special.* But when I entered the formal dining room last night and Thayne laid eyes on me, he'd stared for a long moment, pausing to check me out. His eyes started at the top of my head, moving to my face and then my chest and down to my legs and feet. I stood there, letting him look his fill, wondering if I was interpreting this correctly. I thought I saw a flash of lust in his gaze, but then he reverted to the reserved fire lord.

Maintaining my "I'm just his underage ward" façade is going to be a thousand times harder now that I've spent even more alone time with him, chatting and eating and laughing. I love being with him and I was sad to return to my room last night, alone.

Milli is already taking care of bigger cleaning projects around my suite, so I get up and head into the bathroom to get cleaned and dressed. After I step out of the cleansing unit, I put my robe back on for a moment and walk into the dressing area. The glamour of the stocked closet full of designer Hyrrokin clothes fitted just for me never gets old. I can't seem to allow myself to slip into my old ways of dropping dirty clothes onto the floor and tossing cheap jewelry on any available surface. Mainly because cheap jewelry doesn't exist anymore.

I carefully open a lined drawer and select today's underwear and then pick out my clothes from the lighted racks. Today I decide on soft, stretchy dark pants and another tube top, but this time in a pale pink. Then I slip on some comfortable pink flats that exactly match the shirt. Gone are the days of baggy clothes.

Everything in my closet is tailored to skim my body while remaining stretchy and perfectly comfortable. I put on a pair of simple, sparkly earrings and bypass make up.

I'm hoping that today I'll end up leaving the room again to explore the mansion.

I walk back out and sit in a chair with my tablet on my lap, eating breakfast and drinking Traq from the nearby tray. Milli is still there, and we strike up another conversation. I love chatting with her; she's easy to talk to. She tells me stories about her life, and I discover she's the youngest child from a very large family. I learn about each of her brothers and sisters and what they are doing now that they've all grown up. It's fascinating.

"Do you like living here at the manor?" she suddenly asks me.

"Oh yes, how couldn't I?" I answer honestly with a wave of my hand at all the gorgeous furniture and decor.

She laughs and crouches down in front of the fireplace. "The manor *is* a historic masterpiece. I feel blessed to walk these same halls where so many Hyrrokin have stepped. I have lots of friends from back home who are jealous that I get to work here."

"I can imagine. But…can I tell you something?"

"Of course."

"I…I think Barnabas doesn't like me," I admit to my personal maid, because I'm a people pleaser. It bothers me when people don't like me for unknown reasons. It will probably haunt me to my last breath that Jaden, Maya, and their mother all secretly detested me. Mainly because I'd tried so hard to charm them, and they were having none of it.

I've made sure to try and befriend the staff I've interacted with the most since I've arrived. To get to know the chef, the housekeeper, the stylist, and Milli. The head chef was easy. All I had to do was stop by the kitchen last night and thank him personally for all the amazing food he's made for me since I arrived. I found him pacing the floor of the kitchen, unable to leave and go to bed for the evening because he wanted to know what the new Lady Ashmoor thought of his menu. How sweet was that? I thanked him profusely, letting him know I loved everything and especially the blood pudding. He invited me back to the kitchen anytime I liked.

The other staff I encounter are always warm and polite. But Barnabas is stiff as a board and I think he avoids me. Yes, he was laughing last night at my comments about money management, but I felt more like he was laughing at me, not with me. I don't know what I've done to annoy him, which is bothersome. "Maybe it's because I'm human?" I ask tentatively. "Does Barnabas feel uncomfortable around my species?"

Milli sits back on her heels. "No, no, I'm certain that's not the reason. No one here cares that you're human. Actually, we all think your species is adorable."

My mouth drops open. "You do?"

"Yes," she chuckles and bends down on her knees to clean out the antique fireplace. "It's fun watching you walk around without a tail, balancing on those coverings you wear on your feet. I'm certain Barnabas is wary of you because he's still traumatized by what happened with the first Lady Ashmoor. You'll win him over soon enough though."

"Do you mean Thayne's mother?" I question. "Barnabas didn't get along well with the dowager?"

"No, that's not who I meant. I never got to meet the dowager before she passed, which makes me sad because everyone adored her. Barnabas didn't get along with Lady Ashmoor, the fire lord's former bound."

I sit up straight and put down my tablet. "Thayne was married?"

Milli wipes her dirty gloves on her apron. "Yes, Lord Ashmoor was mated before. You didn't know? His bound died…I think it was three years ago, as did his son. In the great fire of '05. It was really, really sad. His bound and his son both died that night in the fire. And little Lord Wylik was only three years old. It was a terrible tragedy."

"Thayne had a son?" I choke.

Her red brow furrows. "They haven't told you much, have they?"

"No," I squeak, "apparently not." I realize then that I've learned much about Ashmoor history and the manor and their ancient ancestry. The books have been a great resource and the vid classes on Ashmoor etiquette I found on my new tablet are great, but I've only learned about the manor and the history. I know little about the present residents. Thayne always asks me about myself, but he's said little about himself. I'd assumed he hadn't married or had children yet because I'd thought he would've told me something so important about himself. Right?

Last night he'd encouraged me to go on and on about myself and I told him about my mother, my grandparents and my former fiancé. I opened up about my hopes and dreams, and not once did I ask him details about his personal life. Ugh. I'm a bad friend.

"Well, not that I know much either," Milli sighs as she hefts the grate and cleans below it, "I've only been working here at the manor for the last few moon cycles, but I've heard that aristocrats don't always get to declare for the bound they love. Everyone here is much more knowledgeable about it than me. I only got this job because my grandmother once worked here; they like to hire legacy staff. But I heard that aristocracy as well as royalty have to mate with whomever is deemed proper for the greater good of their line."

"Oh, no, that's terrible."

"Right? The rest of us on Tarvos are raised knowing that one day if we meet someone we fall in love with and want as our bound, we can declare for that being and then we are life-long mates. Until then, we can pleasure mate to our heart's content. Well, beings like the fire lord have to carry on his line, which is really ancient. So…" She lowers her voice. "I think what usually happens is that members of the nobility wait until they are right on the line, when they have to declare for a bound and create offspring, or they will run out of time because they'll both be too old for making infants. And meanwhile they pleasure mate. I've heard that sometimes they fall in love with the Hyrrokin who was meant to be their real bound but can't declare for him or her. It's pretty tragic. I don't know why they continue on like that. Sounds so old-fashioned to me."

My mind flashes back to my silly daydreams wherein I imagine that I'm actually Thayne's bound and…and pregnant with his baby. But now I know I can't ever be his bound because I'm human. A fire lord can't have half-human, half-Hyrrokin offspring. It would mess up their ancestry.

"I never met the first Lady Ashmoor, the former bound," Milli continues, "because this was before my time, but I hear that the entire staff hated her."

I scoot my chair closer. "What? Why did the staff at Ashmoor hate her? What did she do?"

"Well, remember that first day when you arrived, and you stepped forward and greeted everyone on the steps? You shook all of our hands, even the two interns?"

"Yes."

Milli stands up and wipes her brow. She smiles down at her handiwork—the perfectly clean fireplace with a brand-new set of ebony logs. "Well, you probably don't realize this, but that was important. It's a big deal to the staff here, that formal meeting. Those two interns at the end that you hugged—the two children—those were Grimwall's two grandsons. So believe me, you got on her good side immediately. I guess that initial introduction is always noted in the history of the ancestry or some such, and well, the first Lady Ashmoor, she didn't finish the introduction like you did. The dowager had to accompany her to get her to greet the staff and she still didn't finish. She said she was tired and stopped halfway through, even though she wasn't tired at all. So that was a terrible beginning. Even so, everyone would've forgiven her, especially if she really was tired or sick, because that's totally understandable, but she continued to be mean to everyone after that."

"Oh wow. How…was she mean? What did she do?"

"Well, she never thanked anyone for their hard work. She berated staff publicly for any mistakes. She complained to Lord Ashmoor that Grimwall was lazy. I heard she used to routinely destroy ancient antiquities with her rough treatment. She also never, ever cared or bothered learning about the Ashmoor ancestry. Plus, she wasn't a very attentive mother. She could go a whole week without seeing her child." Milli takes a step closer, "Sorry, I went on and on there. I promise I'm not normally a carrier of gossip, I only tell you this so you'll understand if any of the other staff are stiff around you at first. They've been burned before and might be waiting to see for sure that you're a nice being who has the best interests of the manor and of the fire lord at heart before they fully trust you."

"I understand." And really, I do.

She smiles down at me, "I trust you already," she remarks.

Aaaw. A matching smile for her widens across my own face.

10

CHARLOTTE

Two hours later I'm bored and ready to do something other than read more print books from the basket Barnabas sent. I'm already on Module 5 on the Ashmoor ancestry vid courses I've accessed through my tablet, so I'm making progress. But again, I'm ready for a break.

I've learned a lot about the manor and Ashmoor history. But I need to get out and gain more applied knowledge. Plus, I've been inside far too long. Stepping out into the manor last night gave me a taste of freedom and I want more. I glance out the window. Two suns and fresh air sounds fabulous. And I'm dying to stroll along the walkways of the formal gardens carved out of the jungle and identify these plants that are similar and yet so different to the ones I'm used to on New Earth.

I'm addicted to landscaping and gardening, although there's not much of that where I live. Mainly container and hydro planting. New Earth was a giant ghetto of kidnapped and enslaved humans for a thousand years until we were freed from the Hurlians. Now my home planet is doing well with an influx of new beings, freedom and currency. There's so much building going on it's crazy, everywhere you look in Singapore there is a skyscraper going up.

Xeno-gardening has become my hobby. I like studying the different flowers and vegetation on the home planets of other species and seeing if I can recreate conditions and get any of it to grow on my own planet. I'd just finished my second year at university. The semester ended one week before the wedding. Next year I was planning on starting a degree in xeno-botany, but I was hoping to transfer to another off-planet university as soon as possible.

I look out through the windows again, wishing I was on the ground, touching and smelling those blossoms instead of admiring them from a distance. I have an itching need to catalogue the varieties in this garden. I recognize the vegetation they've used as border plants, but most everything else I've never seen in my life.

I stand up and put away my books. Last night I found my way to the first floor and was then escorted to the dining room, I suspect I can find it again. I know my room and where the nursery wing is, and my way to the formal dining room and back. That's it. But now I have plenty of clothes to wear so I can go outside too. And I'd love to explore the mansion and the grounds. I don't really want to always stay here having all my meals alone in my room. I'd like to meet up with more of the staff. Maybe eat breakfast with them in the kitchens? Or take more meals in the dining room with...

And, yes, it would be great to run into Thayne again. My chest squeezes at how he lost his bound and three-year-old son in a terrible fire. I glance over at the connecting door and shake my head. I haven't been able to figure him out, but maybe learning about his heart-rending past explains his behavior? I'm his ward, but when we first met he held my hand like we were boyfriend and girlfriend. Then we stepped inside of the manor and he became cold and distant. At dinner he was a changed man. Attentive, talkative, wanting me to sit right by his side and asking me about myself. And he made a date for us to go out together again tonight. But the moment dinner ended he went back to cool and reserved. He blows hot and cold, literally. Is this because he's a widower and in mourning, not yet ready to fully move forward with a new relationship? I don't know.

Or, is it because he's not really that into me?

I have no idea where he went after he ate dinner, but I know he didn't go back to his room right away. I went to the kitchens and then back upstairs. He went in the opposite direction, to somewhere on the first floor. I think? For all I know he could've left the manor to visit someone. In fact, he must've come back so late, I was asleep and didn't hear him. And now he's gone so early I don't know when he woke up and left. Maybe he never even came back to his room and slept somewhere else last night?

A flash of pain spears my chest. What if he went to a girlfriend's house and spent the night? Is that why he didn't return? Maybe Thayne woke up this morning, naked, in another woman's bed?

Ugh. I stand up and stomp towards the door.

I really, really need to go for a walk and get a change of scenery. These silly dreams wherein I become Thayne's girlfriend, or…or what, his wife, are just ridiculous. It's not going to happen. Wishing for something that will never occur will lead to heartbreak. One day he'll finally be ready to remarry, to another Hyrrokin aristocrat, and they'll create strangely adorable, firebreathing Hyrrokin babies of noble ancestry together.

I'm only here to learn about the Hyrrokin species and the Ashmoors in general and one year from now, when I'm considered a legal adult on Tarvos and able to gain my inheritance, I'll move out. This isn't my permanent residence, and this isn't *my* room. I'm a guest—a visitor. Like I'm leaving to study abroad for a year. That's it.

And even if I'm right and Thayne *is* attracted to me as I am to him, he can't act on that because I'm his ward and from a different species. He's a male of honor who would never break the law by touching an underage female. And I admire this about him. So, I have no right to feel angry or jealous over the fact that he's probably continuing with his life and has girlfriends on the side. There will be nothing between us but close friendship, no matter how much I might want more. Meanwhile, I get to live in a luxurious, historic mansion and gain first-hand knowledge of Ashmoor traditions. This is certainly no hardship.

It's not Thayne's fault that I can't get enough of his veiny forearms and his perfect chest. The more time I spend with him, the less he looks like a demon and the more like a handsome fire lord. The black horns that erupt from either side of his forehead now seem stately. His crooked nose is patrician. And when he smiles at me, exposing his sharp fangs, he's dazzling. I ignore the forked tongue and all I see is a man with soft black lips I want against mine.

Last night I lay in bed with my panties so wet I had to get up and change. Then I went to bed and masturbated to the idea of his tongue on my clit and his red cock filling me up. Thayne over me, his black horns in the air above my head and the pointed end of his tail in my hand as he enters me. He'll be so big and heavy, and I think his cock would be bigger than anything I've ever seen or felt.

Then of course I had to get up and change my panties again. It's so very difficult to keep my mind off of him when I'm so very attracted to him.

Enough.

I step out and leave the dowager suite, determined to not fret over my guardian. After a long walk down two different hallways, I stop again at the door of the room that upset Thayne.

Five minutes later and I'm already thinking of him again.

This room was his son's bedroom. After Milli left this morning I checked the Ashmoor ancestry again and learned that

Wylik Ashmoor was indeed, only three years old when he died. I step forward and place my palm on the door, my heart heavy. Now I know why Thayne looked upset when we visited the nursery. This door was directly next to the room I was being shown. Maybe he normally avoids this room, and this entire hallway, because the memories are still too raw?

I wonder what Thayne's son looked like. He must've been darling. It breaks my heart that Thayne lost his little boy. He's a widower who lost not only his wife and son, but a year later, his mother also passed away. We're both living without family.

I saw that he also has a brother, Bane Ashmoor, who is a fire-biologist? But his brother is unmated and doesn't live here and is super busy out in the wildlands. Milli didn't even mention Sir Bane, so I assume he rarely makes it back to the mansion and lives elsewhere. Hopefully he will return for holidays? I'd love to meet this male who is so accomplished in his field of study.

But this means Thayne is without any close family nearby. He is the head of his large extended family, but he seems remote. He hasn't mentioned anyone else coming to the manor to visit or anyone he wants me to meet. Maybe he's keeping himself isolated due to mourning?

I leave the nursery and keep walking and make my way down the grand staircase. My shoes tap on the white marble and my hand rests on a smooth bannister carved like the scales of an undulating dragon. When I look left and right, I can see two long arched hallways that stretch on forever, pointing to either wing of the house. I go forward into the echoing front foyer and keep my gaze on the front doors I entered when I first arrived. I really want to step outside and explore that tantalizing view I've seen out my window.

Okay, maybe I should've told Milli or Grimwall that I was doing this, but I like the idea of being able to explore on my own, when the mood strikes me. I plan on doing more of this—getting to know all the nooks and crannies of the mansion, but first, I want to understand the grounds. I saw the manicured jungle on my way in when I first arrived, and I was enchanted.

An imposing male porter dressed in formal Ashmoor livery stands at the front door, his black horns gleaming in the sunlight streaming from the skylights. All the front windows are open, letting in a perfumed breeze. "Good morning," I smile and lift my chin and keep striding forward across the stone floor, letting him know that I'm going out.

A sliver of worry enters my mind—what if he denies me and that's when I learn I'm in a gilded prison?

But he opens the door and graciously waves me out and in seconds I'm standing on the grand front step with the sweeping vista of the formal gardens. The door closes behind me and pressure lifts from my chest and a smile slashes across my face. It's nice to know they trust me enough to give me the freedom I want.

I stop for a moment and gaze in awe at the vista, suddenly wishing I'd brought the tablet with me, so I could pause to take pictures of this blue sky that reaches out to the horizon.

The steps I originally arrived on are in front of me, but this time I'm alone and I walk down them slowly, remembering what happened when I arrived and how many beings were standing here that day. I study the stone on the steps as I go down.

At the base I'm amazed by the length of each wing of the manor. And then I turn around and take in the majesty of the front façade of the manor. The windows for my own room are on the left in the top floor. Well, wait, I guess I'm on the second floor. Maybe the third floor is where the staff live? How many of the employees live on site and how many go home at night? Interesting. I'll have to ask Milli later.

I turn back around and step down farther, crossing the cobblestoned driveway and walking along the main path to the garden. There are benches lined along both sides of the pathway. A team of Hyrrokin are working on a reflective pool, placing dark stones around the edge and filling up the interior with more water from a hose that is connected to a spout embedded in the ground. I stop to greet them and chat with them about their work.

And then a familiar-looking Hyrrokin female approaches me. She's wearing dark utilitarian trousers and a dark green tube top. The weather is always perfect outside so I can see why none of them wear long sleeves or shoes. Also, if they get cold, I assume they can create their own heat.

"Good morning, Trylia," I say, proud that I remembered her name. "It's nice to see you again." I guess I was able to remember her name because when I met her and she said her job, I was instantly heady with delight, wanting to meet up with her again.

Trylia greets me warmly and we instantly start a conversation about today's landscape construction.

"I'm really interested in xeno-horticulture," I gush. "I like the plants on my home planet but I'm more interested in what's happening on the other planets. The difference between our plants and yours and how they grow different because of how many suns you have versus how many we have and the difference in your soils and weather… I'm boring you aren't I?"

"Lady Ashmoor, I'm the head gardener. Why would I be bored when you speak of plants? This is my life's work."

My face heats up. "Well, it's just that most people find this boring. I lived in an urban center and could only manage a container garden on my patio. I was trying to find space for a small greenhouse and I wanted to order seeds from Salo to try and raise them at my apartment. It seemed like the best place to start since some regions of Salo have similar weather and soil patterns to New Earth."

She nodded. "Yes, I can see that. Can I show you something?"
"Yes, of course."
"Follow me please."

I follow her down a series of pathways and as we walk, she

takes the time to answer all my questions about the preparations they are making for the rainy season. We make a right turn into dense jungle at the edge of the formal garden. And I discover a huge, hidden greenhouse and a collection of work buildings.

"This is the Ashmoor garden center," she explains proudly as she opens a front door and guides me inside. "Would you like to have some space here to create your own personal garden?"

I suck in a breath. "You'd give me room to plant?"

She laughs. "Of course I would. Any being who is interested in plants is always welcome in this greenhouse." She takes me to the back. "You can have this section over here. It's dusty and old, but you could…"

I clap my hands. "Oh, I'd love to fix it up." And I'm not kidding.

"You can start by planting seeds we have here so you can learn about our vegetation, but I'd be happy to help you order seeds from other planets too. I usually stick with plantings that are historical to this estate and to the climate, but I've often thought it would be fun to see what other plants can grow here from other planets."

"Yes, to compare and contrast."

"Exactly."

And then we sit and plan and I know I've found one of my favorite spots in the entire estate.

Hours later I return to my room at the manor, dirty, sweaty and happy. I strip my clothes off, wash my face and hands and put my robe and slippers back on. And that's when I hear my tablet pinging. I rush over and pick it up. For the first time ever, Thayne is messaging me.

Meet me at the auction at sunset, he says. *Do not be late.*

Yes SIR, your Lordship, I respond, laughing out loud.

Thayne replies with a single admonishment: *Female.*

I laugh again because it's like I can hear his deep voice talking to me. I also like that he takes my remarks in stride. I wait for a moment, thinking he might say more, but nope, that was it—I need to show up at sunset, don't be late.

I start to put the tablet down, but I also see a message arrive from my stylist. Lorki lets me know she's sending a team of Hyrrokin over to get me ready for tonight.

Is that really necessary? I answer. *I think I can do this myself...*

No, you can't. This auction is a red-carpet event.

It is? Wow. Okay, I guess I do need your help.

Yes, you do. You're getting a full body scrub, and your tiny claws colored. I even discovered someone who has worked on human hair before, so we'll make sure that stuff on your head looks good too.

Minutes later Milli brings me a tray for a late lunch, and I eat every last morsel. Then I take a nap because that bed is calling out for me. Later I wake up to a knock on the door and I rub at my eyes and drink only one cup of Traq before Lorki and her team shove me into the cleansing unit.

Originally, I thought I would be getting ready at the same time as Thayne and that he would be in the next room and we would leave together, but I learn that he's already in the city. He had business there all day and is working in his office at Ashmoor Central. Duh, this is why he said to meet him at the auction.

"Which one do you like better?" Lorki asks me.

I spend too much time looking between the gold dress and the red dress. Which one? The gold is sexier, and the red is total class. I love them both. Finally, I go for the sexy gold one because I feel like showing off some skin. The weather here on this planet is so perfect and I normally never get to wear dresses like this.

A make-up artist expertly applies my makeup, and I cannot believe how my eyes sparkle and how full and glossy my lips look. My hair is straight and shiny and smoothed back from my face, allowing a good visual of large gold earrings. They paint my nails and toes a glossy white and I'm wearing gold, high-heeled strappy sandals. I can't believe how glamourous I look.

"I love it," Lorki announces. "You're ready."

"Beautiful," Milli breathes.

"Thank you," I blush.

11

THAYNE

Both suns set, and a large glittering crowd of VIP Hyrrokin gather at the entrance to the charity auction.

"Lord Ashmoor! Lord Ashmoor, look this way. Stand right there!" the paparazzi shout.

I blow out a smoky breath and turn toward them, with my hands in my pockets. I've learned it's best to give them an opportunity for a picture right away, so they'll lose interest and move on to the next arrival. I pose for their pics and finally, the clicks end. The queen has arrived, and the riotous crowd rushes off to document her splendid arrival. I step away and stand removed, in a relatively quiet location, trying not to get sucked into conversations. I'm here at the curb focused on the momentary arrival of my gorgeous, chatty human.

Oftentimes I can convince my brother to accompany me to these types of functions, but as usual he's on the other side of the planet, knee-deep in some remote jungle, collecting data on the migration of fire-beasts. Bane is a fire-biologist with zero interest in the Ashmoor corporation. He works hard in his chosen field and has enhanced the Ashmoor brand amongst the scientific and academic communities. My brother is known for his own accomplishments—and I'm proud of him. But he's also unmated, so I haven't yet told him about Charlotte because I want her to myself. I don't know what I'm going to do with this female for now, and once she comes of age, the difficulty in decision-making will increase. But I want her. I can't have her because it is not in my destiny to have more offspring or a female who is legally mine. But I still want her...

Finally, an Ashmoor luxury vehicle pulls up to the curb and my heart rate increases. My female has arrived.

A driver steps out in formal livery and opens Charlotte's door. A delicate human foot appears on the red carpet, covered in elaborate straps of fabric with a pointy heel at the base, and then her perfectly sculpted leg is displayed. Everyone stops and stares at this unusual perfection. Her legs are not deep Hyrrokin-red, but I admire the shape and glow of her gold-colored skin. She is thick in all the right places. I step forward before anyone else can because she is mine. The driver offers his hand to her, but I brusquely push him aside. I don't want anyone else touching Charlotte but me. She takes my hand instead and, in a moment, she's standing in front of me.

My human flashes a brilliant smile and my chest squeezes. Pleasant sensations swoop across my stomach. The feelings I have for her are dangerous.

I cannot believe how lovely she looks tonight. Her beauty is staggering. She's dressed in a golden gown that cups and pushes her breasts up perfectly, leaving two swells at the top on display. The long straight skirt sweeps to the ground but cuts open in front to expose the length of her shapely legs when she moves. Her arms and shoulders are bare and she's wearing a heavily jeweled necklace that looks familiar.

"I think this necklace and earrings were your mother's," she says, "I hope that's okay. The stylist said you'd okayed for me to use it. I hope that was right... It's so beautiful it seems a shame to keep it hidden away..."

MICHELE MILLS

I reach out and finger the glittering necklace, rubbing my claw on her warm skin in the process. The slope of her shoulders and neck are delicious. I want to scrape my forked tongue along her delicate human skin. She sucks in a breath at the charged contact of my claw on her skin, and I feel my cock thicken in my trousers.

"I ordered the vault opened," I rasp, forcing myself to lower my hand, "and a choice of jewelry brought to you in case you wanted to use any of the Ashmoor family jewels. It looks perfect on you."

My former bound wanted only new jewelry, crafted by the trendiest new designers, leaving the "ugly" family jewels locked away. I am pleased to see a necklace I recognize as one of my mother's favorites, passed down for generations, worn today on Charlotte.

She beams up at me. "You look handsome."

"You are beautiful."

Color deepens along her cheeks. "Thank you for saying that. No one has told me that before today."

What is wrong with the males on her planet?

I take her arm and guide her onto the red carpet. We pause to allow the paparazzi a moment to take pics of us together.

"Lady Ashmoor! Lady Ashmoor! What is it like being a human? Is it true you can't flash-flame?"

"How long are you staying at the manor?"

"How did a human become an Ashmoor?"

Neither of us answer any of their questions. My ward waves and smiles, which is a perfect response. This morning I ordered our PR department to send out an announcement to all the vid news channels, letting them know that Charlotte is my new human ward. She does not realize, but tonight I am introducing her to society, as well as to my entire planet. The queen and the president have already sent her messages of welcome, as have most of the Ashmoors. With some notable exceptions.

HIS HUMAN WARD

We walk past the swarm of clicks and the flash of lights and join the crowds entering the building. I pause to speak with other Ashmoors as well as business acquaintances and I introduce my ward to everyone. Pride warms in my chest as Charlotte greets these Hyrrokin, who are strangers to her, with aplomb. Many of them, I know, are secretly offended by the mere presence of an off-planet female in their midst, disgusted at the idea of a *human* as my ward and a fire-baroness. I watch them carefully, ready to come to her defense if needed. These Hyrrokin can whine and moan about her in the privacy of their own domiciles, but I will not accept any being's outright disrespect.

And then a palm presses against my chest. Who is touching me? I frown because this cold touch is not from my Charlotte. I look down at the smiling, seductive face of a Hyrrokin female who is standing much too close to me.

She tilts her head, displaying the shine of her horns and raises up on her toes. "Lord Ashmoor," she hisses seductively against my ear, "it's good to see you again. It's been too long. I want you to know I'm staying the night at the Four Fires Hotel."

Guilt rushes through me because I assume from her heightened intimacy that we pleasure mated many years ago, but I don't remember her name and I know I should. She hands me a claw-written note of some kind that I do not read. I crumple this message and shove it into my pocket, instantly forgotten.

Then I step away from this uninvited female from my past and place a hand on the small of Charlotte's back. I am here tonight with my human and all I see is her. I continue inside with my ward, and I grab two flutes of fire-bubbles from the tray of a passing wait staff, one for each of us. Charlotte squeals adorably at the flash of flame sparking in her glass. I blow out the fires for the both of us and encourage her to sip at her warm drink.

"Oh, it's wonderful." She smiles. "Thank you."

I gaze at her plush lips for far too long, wishing they were around my cock.

"Thayne...Thayne?"

I want her and only her. No other touch will do. I take her hand again, willing my raging lusts to subside. "Follow me." I walk her over to our assigned table.

She looks around with surprise. "We're assigned to be seated at the head table?"

"Yes. I'm always placed at the head table of every societal event."

"Ah."

Relatives join us and we all stand next to the table and chat. I am pleased to see my favorite aunt, her bound and a few distant cousins. It has been far too long since I've seen or spoken to these Hyrrokin. I introduce them all to Charlotte and they immediately accept her with genuine kindness. They ask my ward questions about Targek's passing and I learn my aunt's bound knew Targek Ashmoor because they were both stationed together in the military long ago. And then the subject turns to Charlotte's human age versus her Tarvos legal age, which is the source of all my troubles.

"I will be twenty years old in a few days," she tells them.

"Her birthday is this weekend." I specify because I have already planned a party for her. Well, the staff has planned a surprise party for her, and I'm invited.

"Oh really? My daughter is just a few years older than you," my aunt says, "she's about to give birth to my first grandchild any diurnal now."

"Orcil is pregnant?" I exclaim. I cannot believe how time has flown. Orcil's Bound Declaration ceremony was held just a few months prior to my mother's sudden death from heart failure.

My aunt laughs and places a gentle hand on my forearm. "Yes, Thayne. Your first cousin is about to have a baby any day now. That's why she isn't here tonight. In fact, she's carrying twins!"

There's a tap on my shoulder. "Lord Ashmoor, can I speak to you alone for a moment about an urgent business matter?" I turn toward the serious face of my personal lawyer, Kyrus. I do my best to hide my grimace. It never ceases to amaze me how this male manages to get himself invited to everything and thinks nothing of finding me at these functions to talk business.

"Now?" I motion toward my female, who is laughing at an exchange with my mother's favorite sister. It's obvious they have become fast friends.

"Yes, it's *urgent*."

I frown because even though this male is an amazing lawyer and a committed professional, I've learned long ago that his version of "urgent" and mine are not one and the same.

And I don't want to be separated from my female.

The crowd is full of Hyrrokin who are only pleasant to Charlotte because I'm next to her, teaching them that I will suffer zero disrespect for this human under my care. If any of them cause her a moment's pain, I will char them with my own personal flame. In the future, when they are used to her and she has made many friends amongst them, and they fully understand my expectations, I know she will be fine. But right now, she knows none of them and only has me for support and protection.

I glance around. And also, every unmated male in the room has been gazing lustfully at my female, their eyes lingering on her curves, awaiting their chance to swoop in and speak with my human. I know they want her only as a temporary pleasure mate and not as a bound. The thought of these males trying to turn Charlotte's head and claim her as their own but not give her what I know she eventually wants—love and a family of her own—causes heat to roil in my chest.

And yet, isn't that what I want from her too? Am I any better than these other males? My jaw clenches as I struggle with this ethical dilemma. They don't want to formally mate Charlotte because nobles only want pure Hyrrokin offspring, of the best lines. I don't care about that in the least. I can't ever have Charlotte as my bound because…

Charlotte stands beside me. "Go ahead and talk with him, Thayne. This sounds important." She waves a dismissive hand at me and sits down at her assigned seat at the table. "Don't worry. I'll wait here for you until you come back."

A growl rumbles in my chest. I meet my aunt's gaze and she nods in understanding. Gurcil sits down next to Charlotte. "And I'll stay here with your ward while you're gone," she tells me. "I'd love a chance to get to know her better."

Charlotte smiles and leans forward, seeming to have already forgotten me, continuing her conversation with the older female.

I stare at them both for a moment.

This is acceptable. I nod at Kyrus and follow him into a side room.

12

CHARLOTTE

Thayne's aunt is lovely.
She's a Hyrrokin master gardener, showing me pictures on her tablet of her recent plantings. I'm in awe of her mad gardening skills and I'm thrilled that she's taking the time to talk to me.

Gurcil is in the midst of another hilarious story about her prized fire-blossoms, burnt by stinking beetles, when her tablet starts blinking. "Oh sorry, I need to check this because..." And then she gasps and meets my troubled gaze. "My daughter just went into early labor. She's on her way to the hospital."

"Oh no."

"Sh...she's supposed to be induced next week. I...I've got to go..." She stands on shaky legs.

I stand too and help pull her chair out, making sure she isn't forgetting anything in her haste.

Gurcil looks around at the crowds and bites her lip with two large fangs. "I see a few Hyrrokin around here I don't like. But I've got to go. Make sure you don't leave this table until Thayne returns. Okay? Just stay right here and you'll be fine. He'll be back in a few minutes and if you need anything just message him. Give me your code..."

I hand her my tablet and I receive hers in return and we quickly tap in each other's codes.

"I promise I'll contact you later. Give Thayne my apologies."

I hug her goodbye. "Don't worry about me. Just go and get to your daughter." Then she disappears in the crowd, ready to go find her husband and leave for the hospital.

I sit back down, feeling bereft. I know I don't know Gurcil that well and I've never met her daughter, but I'm worried all the same, and I hope everything turns out well.

I have to admit, it's odd being alone at the auction. The large, elegant room is now jam-packed with loud conversations and thick, powerful, red-skinned beings who all look like Satan, and the occasional flash of flame. But this is a charity auction and a fancy dinner. Nothing to be scared of here, right? Thayne will return shortly. It *is* strange being the only human in a room full of Hyrrokin. There isn't a single being, other than me, who isn't Hyrrokin. Gurcil and Thayne must both be worried that I'll have meltdown over being the only human?

I lift my chin. This will be fine. I've been on Tarvos for a few days now and I've met a lot of Hyrrokin and even though this species might look like a human's worst nightmare, I've learned all their good qualities and I know how noble they are. The humans on New Earth would be lucky to have Hyrrokin as allies.

Is this why Targek married a human? He saw too that we're similar and learned the good qualities of humans? Targek loved my grandmother so much he moved to New Earth to be with her, which was risky because of the Hurlian domination at the time, and he lived out in the middle of nowhere with her so as to not scare the rest of humanity. I still can't believe he sacrificed so much. I do not even know how they managed to meet since she was living on a locked down planet and the Hurlians were still kidnapping humans for their depraved experiments. But they met and Targek stayed with her—maybe protecting her and my mother from the Hurlians? My grandmother loved a Hyrrokin with all her heart, and Targek loved her in return.

This of course causes me to think longingly of my own Hyrrokin, the male I wish was mine, but can't have. My guardian, Thayne Ashmoor.

A few other Hyrrokin sit down on the other side of the table in their assigned seats. I'm usually the type of person who can strike up a conversation with a stranger because I like talking to other people and learning all about them.

They smile at me, and I smile back, but before I can lean forward and introduce myself someone sits in the empty seat right next to me. I glance over, startled, because this is Thayne's assigned seat. And then I frown because I quickly realize it's that annoying female I saw earlier who was giggling too hard and putting her palm against Thayne's chest and leaning in to whisper in his ear. She'd literally pushed me aside to get that close to him. And from the sultry look in her eyes, I'd known that they were pleasure mates. And of course that knowledge burned like a knife in the heart. But I'd managed to keep smiling and pretend like it didn't happen. I have no say in who Thayne dates; it's none of my business. He's single and I'm single. I'm only his ward and I need to remember that.

The female sits down like she owns the place. "I see that you're alone and I wanted to introduce myself. I'm Vitalia Softstone."

"It's nice to me you," I lie. "I'm Charlotte Cruz Ashmoor." I'm suddenly very used to adding my new last name on the end.

She frowns. "I heard them call you Lady Ashmoor."

"Yes, I guess that's my new title? I'm not really used to it yet."

"Oh, you're delightful," she hisses with animosity. "Not even understanding the weight of your title. What a beautiful child."

My nails bite into my palms. "I'm not a child."

"Oh, how old are you?"

"Nineteen," I grit.

"Isn't that…a child? I'm confused."

"On New Earth I'm considered an adult at eighteen. Technically I'm not of age on Tarvos because I'm nineteen still, but I turn twenty in five diurnals."

"Oh, but even after you turn twenty, you're still not going to be legal to inherit for another year so that's why you're Thayne's ward, right? And Thayne is so honorable, I'm certain he won't touch you."

I suck in a breath. "Of course he won't touch me. Why would he? Neither of us will touch each other. There will be no touching." Well, except for holding hands. And the occasional brush of skin on skin. Darn it. Now I feel like a liar.

She looks at me like I'm stupid, then she leans in close and tags me with a harsh gaze. "I know you want him. It's obvious to everyone that you lust after him. I could smell your arousal for him from across the room, but he's mine. You can't have him."

Heat blooms across my cheeks. Holy hell, the Hyrrokin can all smell my arousal? That means Thayne can smell it too? He's known all along that I want him? "No…no," I try to deny, "You're mistaken, I don't—"

Her eyes narrow. "Thayne Ashmoor was in *my* bed last night."

"W…what?" I question, totally caught off guard. Is she saying—

"Yes, you heard me right. I'm telling you I fucked Thayne Ashmoor last night. That male is my avowed pleasure mate. I know you're young and new here, so I wanted to let you know to not bother trying to chase after him. You need to look elsewhere."

Breaths burst in and out of my chest. I have to get away from this bitch.

I rise from my seat and practically sprint away, without looking back, blindly striding forward. I make my way through the crowd, bumping against large Hyrrokin in my haste. Wow, it's like I'm back on New Earth all over again. Is this female somehow friends with Maya Johnson and I don't know? Ugh. I can't deal with this.

And then I stop in my tracks because I overhear a group of females plotting about bedding Thayne. What. The. Hell. I'm standing right behind their backs, and I can hear every word they say.

"...I heard the fire lord never invites anyone to the manor anymore," a female whines. "It's not fair. His bound died so I thought I'd get a chance at him again, but he never shows up at clubs or parties. Then he turned into a shut-in ever since his mother died. All we get nowadays are rare appearances at charity auctions and that damn Fire Ball, which hardly anyone gets invited to anymore. Tonight is our only chance."

"I got all dressed up and came here tonight only because I heard the fire lord was going to be here, alone. Can you believe he brought a human with him?"

They all hiss and groan, clearly angry at my sudden appearance at the event.

I should walk away. I know I should. I don't need to hear any of this but instead I lean in closer.

"And she's technically his ward. What does that even mean? What is she to him? Is he going to mate her?"

There's a snort of disgust. "I'm sure they've already pleasure mated."

"No! She's still underage."

"So? Jusical was standing so close to them she said she could *smell* the human's arousal for Lord Ashmoor."

My stomach clenches at the general gasp of surprise from the group.

"And I heard she's legal this weekend. Maybe they didn't want to wait."

"But she's only been living with him for a few days..."

"That doesn't matter. You give me one diurnal in that mansion and I'd have my mouth on his flaming red cock too."

They all chuckle with delight at that remark and nod in agreement

I have to admit I understand why they want him so much. I can see the difference between Thayne and other males. All the males are bare-chested and barefoot; they all wear tailored black pants. But there is something special about the heavy, ornate silver buckle on Thayne's belt. And he's got on that black silk sash with the Ashmoor crest he always wears across his chest when he goes out. Tonight, it's even nicer than usual, with the family motto and jewels embedded into the coat of arms.

His chest is so hard and defined and his waist is utter perfection. I stare often at the movement of his ass. And those epic thighs. And his forearms...I swoon over his forearms. But I think it's not simply that he's probably the epitome of Hyrrokin male handsomeness—he's also got this aura of aristocratic arrogance about him that isn't fake. He's the real deal. He can back up all that arrogance.

I haven't heard any of the other males referred to as "fire lord." I think...I think he might be the only "fire lord" on Tarvos? Which is special. That must be why the paparazzi were taking so many pictures of him when we entered. And it would be even more heartbreaking for traditionalists on this planet, if this fire lord who represents their culture marries a *human*.

"I don't even know if I'd want to be his bound," one of the females sniffs. "That ancient manor and that straight jacket of Ashmoor tradition is a lot. Too many *rules*."

"Hells, no," another exclaims, "but I wouldn't mind for a second being his avowed pleasure mate. That way you'd get plenty of expensive gifts, lots of hot sex and zero responsibility."

"Right? Perfect."

They all laugh. And suddenly I feel bad for Thayne.

"But first, we've got to find a way to get rid of that human. She's a triple threat—sexy, cute and unmated. Having her here means none of us can get him alone. What are we going to do?"

"Maybe we can spike her drink?" someone says, "or push her off the stage."

"Oh, I've got a better idea how about if we..."

I walk away because now they're plotting my demise. They're out to get me because I guess they consider me a threat? It's crazy.

I stumble toward the bathroom, trying to keep my tears at bay. Holy crap, why didn't anyone tell me how intensely the females on Tarvos consider Thayne a good catch? My first mistake was telling Thayne that he could leave me alone. But how was I to know Gurcil would be called away by a family emergency? And how was Gurcil to know that bitch would take Thayne's seat?

I make it into the bathroom, trying to be alone so I can cry in peace. I really don't want to go out there again. I dart past the stalls and the mirrors, where there are lots of other Hyrrokin females chatting. I know I shouldn't let those bitches out there get to me, but they do. Just like with the Johnsons, they know my pain points and are exploiting them—It's true that I'm a human and technically underage. And I'm living with a male who all the women want and who I can't have. And maybe I'm not worthy of him?

And...and Thayne really does have a girlfriend he was pleasure mating last night. It's terrible to have my vague suspicions confirmed. I thought I was worrying over worst case scenarios, but nothing real.

Instead, nope, it was totally real.

Ugh. I push through another door and find myself in a quiet, dimly lit salon in the back that appears empty. Thank gods. I sink down onto the nearest plush chaise and drop my head into my hands.

He's my guardian and I'm nothing but his ward. I know I have no right to be hurt, as if I were betrayed or something—but the fact remains that the thought of him with someone else makes me want to scream. And those words from the females in the crowd aren't helping matters.

What am I doing to bring this negativity onto me? I always try my best to put kindness out there into the universe. Why am I not getting that same energy reflected back to me? Again and again, I seem to draw mean people straight to me. Why?

Tears track down my cheeks.

"Human, what's wrong?" a kind voice questions.

I sit up straight. What the heck? Another Hyrrokin female, who is dressed super fancy, is sitting on a couch in a shadowed corner. "Oh, I'm sorry" I say. "I thought I was alone in here. I'll go..." I start to stand.

"No, don't go." She moves over to sit down beside me, and I settle back into the seat. Her voluminous yellow skirts brush against my legs. "My name is Rebyka. Tell me what's wrong, so I can help."

She looks about the same age as me, but by the tone of her voice I can tell she's a genuine being, like Gurcil and many of Thayne's relatives I've met tonight. And like all the females I've met at the manor.

I look into her sparkling black eyes. "Hi, I'm Charlotte." This female seems truly concerned for me. Plus, she was in here hiding too...so I decide to open up to her. I wave a hand in the general direction of the party we both left. "When I was out there, something happened that reminded of how mean females can be to each other sometimes. It...it just really hurt and I needed to get away for a minute."

She snorts. "Ain't that the truth. Women can be bitches sometimes. It's the worst. That's basically why I'm here too. Sometimes they don't realize we can overhear what they say behind our backs. Which is why I always have this on hand, just in case." And then she pulls out a shiny metal flask, loosens the cap and takes a sip of what I assume is alcohol. She offers it to me. "Want some?"

I don't normally drink hard alcohol, but in this instance I'll make an exception. I smile back, "Sure. Why not?" And I take the flask and toss back probably too much. She pats my back as I cough at the chemical heat that scorches down my throat. Whoa, now I remember why I don't usually do shots. I hand it back to her, "And you know," I rasp, "I feel like this meanness keeps happening to me."

She pouts. "It does? Tell me."

"Well…on New Earth my best friend (I say with air quotes) and her mother were pushing me off onto their brother, wanting me to date him and marry him. I thought it was because they liked me so much, they wanted me as family, but I learned at the last second it was because they wanted to steal my inheritance."

She reaches out and grabs my hand in her soft claw. "Oh, I'm so sorry, that's terrible."

I sniff. "Thank you, but in the end it was okay because I figured out what they were doing before I married my friend's brother. And now I'm far away from them, on Tarvos. But now I'm crying because I just had females I don't even know plotting against me here. I left New Earth and went to another planet to live amongst an entirely different species, and it's happening again. Females still want something they think I have that they don't."

"And what is that?"

I let out a bitter laugh. "Thayne Ashmoor. I'm his new human ward and some of the unmated females here see me as an obstacle because they want him for themselves. I was told by one female that she was fucking him last night and he is her pleasure mate and to back off."

Rebyka's eyes narrow and smoke puffs from her nostrils. "Who said that to you?"

I purse my lips, "I don't want to start more trouble. I mean, if she did have sex with him, all she was doing was telling me a truth maybe I needed to hear. I admit that I really, really like him and that's stupid because I'm underage and human so we can never be together."

She shrugs and takes another sip of her flask. Then she hands it back to me again and I take another sip and pass it back. We're both quiet for a moment and then she says, "I know Thayne. We grew up together. I promise I have no desire to make him my bound or my pleasure mate. To me he's that annoying distant cousin who always took first place in the fire bird competitions. And believe me, he was never humble about it."

A chuckle escapes my lips. "You don't? Well, that's a relief. At least there's one unmated female here who doesn't want him."

We both laugh at how silly this entire situation sounds.

She leans close. "Since you're admitting to me such personal feelings, I'll tell you mine. I'm in love with the female who is the head of our military. But she is not considered noble enough for me to declare for. And it is my duty to birth heirs of good genes to continue my line. I am intended for another, a male of equal social standing and currency. Obviously, I don't want to be his bound."

"Oh shit." I squeeze her hand. "I'm so sorry."

"Me too," she whispers.

We both sit there a bit longer, until we finish the flask. "Well, I guess we should return," Rebyka finally says.

I nod in agreement and rest my head, which feels really, really heavy, against her soft shoulder. "Thank you for listening to me."

She lilts her head against mine. "No, thank you for listening to me, human. You have no idea how refreshing you are."

I scrunch my nose, not even sure how to respond to that.

"I'll leave first," she declares, "and make sure it's all clear for you. Wait here a few minutes after I leave and then you can leave too and go straight back to your assigned seat. I'm sure Thayne will be back by the time you get there."

"Okay." I lift my head and give her a goofy smile. "You can do that?"

"Yes." She grins. "I can. Also, give me your tablet so we can exchange codes."

I hand it over. When we're done entering our codes for each other, we smile, readying to depart. I love the white gleam of her fangs against the black shine of her soft lips. Her necklace sparkles with so many jewels it's like a flash of fireworks. She's actually a very pretty devil.

"Ready?" she questions.

"Ready," I answer.

And then we implement the plan.

13

CHARLOTTE

Minutes later I've returned to the head table.

Rebyka was true to her word—I stepped out after her and the way was clear. And I managed to make it back to my seat with my head high, walking in a reasonably straight line, pretending I hadn't just drunk way too much Hyrrokin alcohol straight from a flask.

Thayne shows up seconds later and I can't hide anything from him. "Who has upset you?" he growls.

Suddenly I'm irritated with him because he's essentially the one who started all of this by being so sought-after and sexy. And then having sex last night with someone who *wasn't me*, after we'd had an intimate dinner together in the formal dining room. I spent the evening baring my soul to him because he'd flirted with me and kept asking me about myself and then he left and went directly to Vitalia and fucked her and slept in her bed? He probably held her in his arms all night, not even remembering my name. And meanwhile I'd spent most of the night awake and alone, listening for his footfall. Finally masturbating so I could get some sleep.

How dare he?

Really. *How dare he?*

I stand back up and get right in his face. "Your girlfriend is the one who upset me," I spit out. "I should go back to the manor. It's silly that I'm sitting here with you instead of her. Why didn't you ask her to come to this auction with you? Why did the two of you arrive separately? Shouldn't she, at the very least, be at our table with us?"

He rears back. "What girlfriend?"

I point back toward the crowd. "Vitalia Softstone, the girlfriend who you spoke to earlier when we first arrived. The one who put her hand on your chest, whispered in your ear and handed you a note. Remember? I'm sure she's still here somewhere. She came and sat with me while you were gone and let me know that she's yours and for me to back off."

"This is ridicu—" He leans down and sniffs at the crook of my neck. "Charlotte…are you drunk? What happened while I was gone? Where is Gurcil? Why did she leave you alone?" He reaches for my hand.

I jerk away from his touch and look him right in the eyes and don't back down. "D…don't touch me," I slur. "Vitalia said she fucked you last night, that you slept in her bed and that she is your avowed pleasure mate."

A growl rumbles in his chest. He leans in and lowers his voice, anger clear in his tone, "I don't care what that female said to you. Listen to me, Charlotte. I do not have a pleasure mate, or a "girlfriend." I have not mated with anyone other than my former bound in the last seven years. I am here with you because you are the female I want to be with. Only you."

I want so badly to believe him, but I'm not sure…my head is spinning. I glance around and notice we're making a scene. Everyone at the table is staring up at us and so are groups of other Hyrrokin. Pointing and whispering. Oh hell. I lick my lips and shift uncertainly on my feet.

He puts his arm around my waist. "We're leaving. You've had enough." Then he starts leading us both away from the table.

"We're leaving? No, no. The auction hasn't even started. Look, they're just starting to serve dinner. This is supposed to be about you giving currency to the Tarvos Wildlife Fire-Animal Fund. I don't want to be the reason animals don't get help."

His lips twitch. "This evening was about me introducing my ward to Hyrrokin society. But I'm not staying if you feel uncomfortable. I want you safe and undisturbed. I'll send a sizeable donation later to the Fund. That's all they care about."

"Oh, okay," I breathe, happy to hear that no animals would be hurt in our sudden exit from the auction. Actually, I'm happy that we're leaving too.

Thayne guides me through the crowd, which parts for our departure. We head outside to the Ashmoor luxury vehicle, which is already waiting at the curb.

"How did the driver get here so fast?"

"My driver was watching from his position at the door. I already motioned to him that I was ready to depart. I often leave early; they are used to this."

The door opens and we enter the vehicle together and sit side by side. It pulls away from the curb and Thayne takes my hand, just like he did when we first left the chapel on New Earth and arrived on Tarvos.

I lean back, my head still spinning and my stomach churning. "I can't believe you were with someone else last night," I continue to rant, because I can't seem to stop myself from vomiting up every single emotion that crosses my mind. And I just can't get past this. "I know I shouldn't care. I told myself not to care because I'm just your underage human ward. It's not like we're together and you were cheating on me or anything. But..." I whimper, "it hurts that we had dinner together last night and then you left and went directly to someone else's bed..."

He places a hand on my thigh and reaches his arm out to pull me in close. Now my head rests on Thayne's impressive shoulder. Why does he always smell so good? Is this a trap?

"Female…" He carefully runs a claw along the tip of my nose and along my cheek. "Female, last night I left the dining room and went to my office on the first floor and worked late into the night. I do that now more than ever just so I won't be tempted to knock on your door and reach for you. I went back upstairs in the middle of the night and opened the connecting door to our rooms and checked on you. I stood by your bed and watched your beautiful sleeping form for a few minutes, assuring myself of your safety, then I walked into my own room and closed the connecting door behind me. I slept fitfully because we were so close and yet apart. I woke up early this morning and left before you awoke because I cannot be near you and *not* touch you. I made it through my workday today without you only because I knew in the evening I would see you again."

Tears burn behind my eyes. "Really?"

"Really. Do you trust my word?"

"Yes." I turn in to his hard red chest, reach out and grab onto his sash. "Thayne, I want you, but I can't have you and it haunts me day and night. I wish I was older."

The Fire Lord of Ashmoor kisses me on the forehead and runs his claws through my hair. "I feel the same, female. The same."

I slump against his chest and we're both quiet for a moment and then I blurt out, "I learned this morning that you were married and had a son and they both died…"

His muscles tighten and his fingers still in my hair. He starts to pull away from me.

I sit up and place a hand on his claw. I'm weepy about this and I can't help it; I have to talk about what happened. I can't pretend I don't know. "I'm so sorry for your loss, Thayne. So very sorry. I went past the nursery on my way downstairs today and I stopped and touched that same door you were staring at the day I arrived because now I know why it was special to you. It was Wylik's room."

He shakes his head and looks away from me. He takes a deep breath. "Yes, that was my son's room. I hadn't been in that passageway in almost three years."

I snuggle back into his side, and he allows it.

"My former bound and my son died on the same night. There has been no one else since. And we were together for four years prior to her death. Females proposition me, but I turn them all down."

"Why?"

"Are you asking why those females proposition me?"

"No, silly, I understand that part. Why do you turn them all down?"

His jaw clenches. "I have trust issues."

"Aaah."

"No, you don't understand. I declared for my bound, and we went to the courthouse and made it official, because it was expected of me. The royal family as well as the aristocracy on Tarvos follow strict traditions of mating from within to keep lineage pure. Letecia Limestone was chosen for me by my parents. The Limestones did not have as ancient lineage as the Ashmoors but she would bring more lands and wealth. It was a good merge. Her line was small and about to atrophy."

"Did you love her?"

"No. I didn't. I tried. My heart was open to her, and I was fully ready to give our relationship my all. She became pregnant right away and I was thrilled to have a child. But she changed soon after she gave birth to our son…"

I wait for him to say more, but instead he changes the subject.

"I have been sending mixed signals to you. The other Hyrrokin understand this. They think that you are more than simply my ward. They think you are my avowed pleasure mate and that I will eventually make you my bound. But you need to know that I will not take another bound, nor will I have offspring. I did that before, and it didn't work out. I did my duty when I took my former bound and I was ready to live a life with a mate I did not love. I was going to never have love and I'd accepted that. But at least I had my son. But I was unable to protect my offspring or choose the correct life mate to be a mother. I do not deserve another chance."

My mind instantly narrows on the most salient point. "Wait, you are never going to marry again?"

"No. All we can ever be is pleasure mates, which isn't fair to you. I will never have more offspring. I plan on leaving the role of fire lord to my brother's offspring or that of a cousin. I cannot turn my lust for you into an actual relationship. I am not ready for another bound and a new offspring. You need to know that."

The vehicle stops at the landing pad and Thayne insists on carrying me in his arms again, which is fine because my head is still spinning. Minutes later we're in the back of the hovercraft, similar to how we traveled together that first day. The craft lifts in the air and all the same needs rise up, literally. I gasp when I see the spike that rises underneath the crotch of Thayne's trousers.

I lick my lips. "This is for me?" Holy crap his penis is enormous, and I want it in my pussy now. I'm drunk and I need sex, right now.

He spreads his thighs and leans back in his seat. "For you. You do this to me," he rasps. "My cock is hard in my trousers, leaking seed, ready to mate. Your scent enters my lungs in the enclosed space. And you're again staring at my forearms and then my abs and down to my tented crotch."

"What are we going to do about it?" I ask because I'm still drunk and my nipples are two hard points of need.

"Nothing."

"Nothing?" I pout.

"You are not of legal age."

I lean back too and spread my own legs, wishing he would help me with this throbbing clit. "My birthday is on Saturday." I remind him.

"Charlotte…" he warns. "I just told you that all we can ever be is pleasure mates and you told me last night your dream is to have a bound and offspring to start your own family. You can never have this with me."

"Maybe I want to pleasure mate?" I widen my legs a bit more and place a hand on my inner thigh, letting my fingers drift close to my panties. Now I'm certain he can see the wet spot on my underwear—I'm so wet for him it's about to leak down my thighs. "I want your cock," I boldly proclaim.

A choking sound emits from his throat. "I can't put you on my cock, Charlotte. You're underage. It would be illegal. And also, you're drunk and not in the right frame of mind to rightfully offer your consent. I just told you that I can never be your bound and you are still trying to mate with me. This is not right. I will not take advantage of you. I will keep you protected, even from me."

I let out a huff of disappointment. "You can put me on your cock five diurnals from now, after I turn twenty."

"No, I can't. After that you are still my ward."

"And because I'm human?"

He shakes his head. "I don't care that you're human."

"The nobility on Tarvos care. They would be disgusted if you ended up with half-human, half-Hyrrokin heirs. I want to be your bound and have your babies, but I can't."

"You're right about the nobility and it displeases me that others in my line feel that way. But I do not care in the least that you are human. I would be lucky to have a female like you as my bound, but I told you, I'm not ever taking another mate because I've vowed to never have more offspring. I can't…"

And then the hovercraft lands and our charged moment in the backseat is over.

Thayne sweeps me off my feet and carries me in his arms through the dark night. The fabric of my dress flutters against my ankles. We go from the hovercraft, along the front terrace of the east wing, up the front steps, and into the manor. I don't say a word the entire time; just lay my cheek against his shoulder, trying to keep from passing out. He adjusts me in his arms, so I'm pressed closer against his chest, then he progresses up the brightly lit grand staircase, through one hall and then another and right to my bedroom door—which is next to his.

He deposits me on my feet and then moves in close.

The heat of his large body is intoxicating. I reach up and cup his terrible face with both of my hands and stare hungrily at his lips. He groans and leans down to capture my mouth with his own. This isn't a delicate kiss, oh no. His forked tongue sweeps inside and my body dissolves with desire. His fangs clash with my blunt teeth.

He pulls me close, so my body is pressed against his own and I stand on my tiptoes and slide my arms around his neck. My hard nipples move against his chest. His claws thread through my hair and he bends me back with the power of his claiming. I feel consumed. Taken.

It's easily the best kiss of my life.

Then he breaks off our fierce kiss and I sway in his arms, panting and confused, my lips kiss-swollen and tender.

Suddenly Milli arrives and Thayne hands me off to my frowning personal maid.

Then his own door clicks open and shut and he's gone.

14

CHARLOTTE

I wake up the next morning feeling like I've been down ten miles of bad road and find a message on my tablet from my new partner-in-crime, Rebyka.

I'm hungover, she tells me.

I groan and immediately sit up, then send back three Hyrrokin sick-looking emoji faces. *Me too, girl. Me too. I feel like fire warmed over.*

But totally worth it? She questions.

Yeah…I got to meet you! That's worth the price of admission right there!

But then everything else that happened last night floods back with embarrassing clarity. Ugh… I fall back into the bed and cover my face with both hands and tear up at my antics.

I got drunk in the ladies salon at a fancy charity auction.

I spread my thighs for Thayne in the back of his hovercraft.

I begged for his cock.

I told him I wanted to have his babies.

He said he wanted me too, but he was never, ever going to marry anyone ever again. And he most certainly wasn't going to have more children.

Then he kissed me within an inch of my life and left me at my bedroom door.

Dear gods.

And...was that a goodbye kiss from Thayne or a "this is the start of something new" kiss? I don't know! How can I possibly talk to him today like none of those things happened last night?

Well, the good news is that Thayne does *not* have a girlfriend, no matter what that bitch at the auction tried to say.

I basically threw myself at him and he did the noble thing and kept his hands off me—well, until that last kiss. But he kept it to just one kiss and then he was gone. I actually kinda appreciate how he was keeping me safe, from him.

On Tarvos, I'm considered underage until four days from now, when I turn twenty. He said he wanted me as more than a pleasure mate, but he feels he can't have me. It's not because I'm too young—that will change this weekend. He doesn't want to marry again after losing his wife and son to that fire. To be truthful I don't understand that part. Maybe this is where my inexperience is the problem. I'm much younger than him and I've never even had a real boyfriend, just two different long-term dating episodes that included meh sex. I don't know what it's like to have lost a spouse and a child at the same time. But I can imagine...and it still does not add up in my mind to never trying again. But that's how he feels.

I sniff up tears as I think about how Thayne and I can't be together. And then I remember my friend who is in the same dilemma with the woman she loves but can't have.

Milli knocks on the door and enters the room.

I roll over and moan. "I feel terrible." My head is pounding, and my mouth is as dry as a desert.

She marches over and fluffs up my pillows for me. "That's what happens when a human drinks too much fire-alcohol. Sit up," she orders and then hands me a glass of water, which I eagerly gulp down.

I whimper, continuing to feel sorry for myself, and pick up the tablet again, needing to talk to the one being who will understand. *I feel terrible,* I message.

Yep. The next morning is always the worst, Rebyka responds. *This is how you fix it...*

And then she sends me exact instructions on what meds to take and what to eat and drink to rid myself of the Hyrrokin fire-alcohol hangover from hell, which I'm learning is the worst kind of hangover. I show Milli the messages from Rebyka and she gets everything for me and helps me follow this prescription to the letter.

In the midst of this, I receive pics from Gurcil of her holding two adorable twin baby boys in each arm. They barely have horns, only black nubs on their heads and their red skin looks velvety soft.

Precious.

I love babies and I'm so happy to learn that everyone in Gurcil's family is healthy and happy. I send back messages of congrats and start secretly planning how to visit Gurcil's daughter and her new twins when she's ready for guests, along with the gifts I'll bring. I'm not sure how to make my way to this female's hospital room, or even later to her domicile, but I'm ninety-nine percent certain if I just ask Gurcil and Grimwall for guidance I can make this meet-up happen.

Thanks so much, I tell Rebyka, checking back in an hour later. *It's working. I feel much better already. How do you feel?*

No prob, human. I feel a lot better too. Hope you have a nice day, my new friend.

You too!

And then I receive a ping from Thayne. He's messaging me again?

I grip the tablet like it's a lifeline. I bite my lip and my pulse quickens because that's how much I love this guy. Oh hell. Love? I've fallen in love with a satanic-looking fire lord who's vowed to never marry again? He's in mourning over the loss of his wife and child. And, even if he was up for marriage, I'm the human who can't help him carry on with his line. Yeah, I foresee nothing but heartbreak in my future and yet I drift right at Thayne like an original planet moth to a flame.

How are you feeling this morning? The male who kissed me last night asks.

I'm good, I answer simply, like nothing untoward happened, even though I vividly remember his tented crotch and how I spread my thighs for him. Jeez. And the feel of his lips on mine. And his erection pressed against my stomach as we kissed.

How is that possible? He questions. *You must be hungover. Do you require a doctor?*

No, I'm fine now. I made a new friend last night and we messaged this morning and she already told Milli exactly what I should take to make it go away. I feel better already.

Is this friend my aunt, Gurcil?

No, someone else. Her name is Rebyka. She's really nice. We met while I was crying in the bathroom. She was sad too over something else, so we were bonding.

Heh.

I wait for another response but it's silent. Then he finally answers. *Well, I'm happy to know you are well and making new friends. I am in the city working today, but I will see you at dinner tonight at the manor.*

I smile. I love that despite his busy day, dealing with his high-powered business dealings, he's checking in to see how I'm doing and still wants to have dinner with me. He's even letting me know his whereabouts and his schedule. This gives me hope that maybe, maybe, despite the obstacles, we might still have a chance?

Then I remember something important I need to tell him. *Thayne? Thayne? Did you know that your cousin, Gurcil's daughter, went into labor last night?*

No...

Yeah, that's why Gurcil left. I'm sorry, I forgot to tell you. I got a message this morning from Gurcil letting me know that her daughter gave birth to two gorgeous baby boys late last night. You have two new second cousins!

I forward the pics to him.

Thank you, he answers.

You're welcome. See you tonight.

MILLI FINALLY LEAVES to attend to other tasks for the day, deciding I'm well enough because I'm eating breakfast like a normal Hyrrokin. After I eat some meat and drink my favorite flavor of Traq, I decide I'm ready to continue with my day too.

I get up, use the cleansing unit and spend extra time with the mouth and teeth cleanser and get dressed in work wear. Then I go down to the greenhouse to check on my plants.

The fresh air, the sunshine on my face and the explosion of beauty all around do wonders for my disposition. I wave good morning to all the gardeners who are out in force, bracing the estate for the upcoming rainstorm. They know the exact day it will start—the day after my birthday. Delicate flowers are being covered. Furniture and umbrellas are brought indoors to storage. Anything that can blow away is being locked down.

I enter the greenhouse and find it empty today of other Hyrrokin—they must all be busy elsewhere, readying for the rainy season. I happily spend the next two hours there, alone, just quietly tidying up my little corner and working on my plants and ordering new seeds. It's lovely.

A growl of hunger rumbles in my stomach, letting me know it's time to leave. Maybe I can go directly to the kitchen and eat lunch there, instead of in my room? Companionship sounds nice right now.

I walk up from the gardens back to the manor and I see a lone vehicle driving up onto the main driveway to park at the base of the steps. Hmm, this is interesting. I'm used to fancy black vehicles parking up front, it's nothing to me. A driver usually jumps out to open the back doors so important-looking Hyrrokin can carefully step out and walk up the grand steps to attend business meetings with Thayne.

But this time an open-air, all-terrain vehicle, with dried mud splashed all over the side panels, boldly parks on the cobblestone driveway and a lone female human steps out of the driver's seat.

I gasp with surprise and walk faster to catch up. This has to be the neighbor Thayne mentioned yesterday.

Yay.

The young woman looks out onto the gardens and catches my gaze and waves at me with a big smile, letting me know she's here for *me*. I wave back and smile in return. To be truthful, I feel like we could be of the same family. Her hair is much longer than mine, and her eyes darker, but she's big and curvy like I am, and we've got a similar skin tone.

"Hi," she says when I get close, "I'm your neighbor, Ariana Gonzalez-Strikestone."

She puts out a hand for me to shake in greeting, but I bypass that and go straight for a tight hug. She laughs and hugs me back.

"Oh my gosh, it's so good to see another human. I can't believe you live next door. Thank you for coming to visit with me."

"Well." She shrugs, pointing off in the distance. "It's weird to say we're neighbors considering our two estates are so large I had to drive here to see you, but still, yes, we're 'neighbors.'"

I laugh at her description and then finally process the enormity of her name. "Wait, did you say your human last name is Gonzalez?"

"Yes, on New Earth I'm known as Ariana Gonzalez the fifth."

"Ariana Gonzalez the *fifth*?" Oh wow, I'm having a celebrity meltdown crush.

"I know, I know." She waves a hand. "But I'm just Ariana, believe me, nothing special."

I have a hard time believing that, but I shut up about it to keep her comfortable.

She frowns at the large gift basket she brought, which is still in her passenger seat. "Darn it, I was told you'd be a young girl, so I brought gifts for a child."

"I know, I know, they all thought that at first." I laugh. "You should've seen the expression on Thayne's face when he arrived on New Earth to pick me up and discovered I was an adult. Don't worry, I'll love anything you brought."

"Even if there are only outfits here for a baby?"

I take the gift basket from her and lean in to whisper, "Thayne has a cousin who just had a baby. I'll regift it all to her, so you're saving me from having to search for a present."

"Oh, perfect."

We walk up the steps together, chatting along the way. I tell her all about how I'm staying for a year and how I'm Thayne's ward. "That reminds me, you have to see my closet. You'll love what they've done." I stop at the front door to the manor, surprised to see it's not already opened for me. Maybe the porter was called away? Well, I guess I'm spoiled. This is no big deal, so I open one of the heavy doors myself and try to guide my guest inside.

"No…no, wait," Ariana shakes her head. "We have to stay out here and chat. I can't go in because I'm a Strikestone. Skoll and Lord Ashmoor are sworn enemies."

I stop in my tracks. "What? No way." The door is still open, and a porter finally arrives and deftly takes the gift basket from my hands and disappears again. I catch a glimpse inside of Grimwall pacing in the foyer. What is up with them?

Ariana remains just outside the threshold. "Yeah, the Ashmoors and the Strikestones hate each other with a fiery passion and have for hundreds of years. It's a historic feud that everyone in this county knows about in great detail. Both families do terrible retaliations and retributions against each other so the feud continues. I think this generation it's a little better though. I mean, Skoll and Lord Ashmoor are at least now on speaking terms. Just me standing here at the estate chatting with you is a huge step forward."

It's still hard for me to wrap my brain around the concept of a feud because this is Ariana Gonzalez the fifth. *The fifth.* "You're their closest neighbor and you've never been inside?"

I glance over at Grimwall, who moves close and gives a tight nod. And then I notice she's acting very formal and not at all like herself. They do all distrust Ariana because she's a Strikestone. It's silly.

The housekeeper steps forward. "Chef has prepared a nice luncheon on the front terrace for you and your guest, if you'd like," she suggests.

"No," I say. "I don't like."

"Lord Ashmoor has expressly prohibited..." she tries to whisper to me. "There's...there's a rule in the ancestry that forbids Strikestones from entering the manor."

I purse my lips and shake my head. "I'll fix this," I tell Ariana.

"Oh, I don't mean to be a bother. It's really no problem. I promise I'm not upset. I knew when I came over to visit that I wouldn't be allowed inside and that this would be a quick visit. I just wanted to see another human face to face."

"You're not a bother. I'm thrilled you're here."

She takes a step back. "I'll go home, and we can message each other later, or you can visit me at the Strikestone lodge."

I pull out my tablet, irritation at Thayne coursing through my veins. "No, that's not necessary. Please stay and have lunch with me. Hold on I'll fix this right now." Some ancient feud is not going to be the reason Ariana Gonzalez the fifth isn't allowed inside the manor.

Ariana Strikestone is here to meet with me, I message Lord Ashmoor.

He answers back immediately. *Skoll's human bound is at the manor?*

Yes, she brought us a gift and I want to have lunch with her, but the staff say they can't let her inside because of some ancient rule about not allowing Strikestones to step foot inside of the Ashmoor manor?

True, there is a rule.

Fix it! I want this rule gone so I can visit with my friend.

And right then I see Grimwall checking her own tablet and smiling down at the message she's just received. She lifts her head and graciously nods at Ariana. "I am so sorry for the delay," she tells my new friend. "Would you do me the honor of coming inside so that we may offer you and Lady Ashmoor a formal luncheon in the dining hall and then provide for you both a tour of the mansion?"

Ariana grins with delight and steps inside the manor with me. The porter closes the door behind us both. "Thank you so much for the offer," Ariana says, "I would love to spend time in the manor with Lady Ashmoor."

I look back down at my own tablet because I have a new message from Thayne: *Done. Have a good day, human.*

Thank you. I appreciate.

You're welcome, female.

I SPEND the next four days finishing more teachable vid modules on Hyrrokin history and caring for my little garden in the corner of the greenhouse.

My corner is looking cute. It started out dank and dusty but after a lot of hard work I've got careful rows of seedlings already started. And I've been spending a lot of time cataloguing all the various flowers grown on the estate. Also, the head gardener has okayed me clipping blossoms from the main gardens to gift to others and create bouquets.

I form a daily pattern. I get up early, get dressed and go down to the kitchen to meet up there with the head chef and help him and his assistants make fresh bread. I eat two fire-scones straight out of the oven, along with plenty of Traq. Then I take my tablet and head into the library, which is on the same wing as Thayne's office and camp there and do my Hyrrokin vid studies all morning.

A treasure trove of print books line the library walls from floor to ceiling, and the windows provide stunning views of the back gardens, which are left wild with vines and purple flowers. The smell of all that paper and ink is heady and the books are a terrific resource. I sit in a comfy chair with my tablet in my lap, in front of yet another stone fireplace loaded with a crackling fire and respond or initiate messages with Thayne, Rebeka or Ariana. But I really do manage to get a lot of studying done.

I eat lunch in the kitchen with the staff because I love their stories about Thayne's youth and their favorite memories of the dowager. The first time I mentioned Lord Wylik they all grew quiet, because I guess they have a hard time talking about him due to his tragic death? But they soon warmed to the idea of telling me stories of the little boy they all loved.

After lunch I always head out to the gardens, because the sunshine and fresh smell of flowers and soil makes everything right. I can't believe how lucky I am to be here. Yesterday I contacted the university on New Earth and canceled my next two semesters. I also let go of my apartment. Thayne hired an inter-planetary moving company to pack my belongings (which wasn't much beyond my luggage that I knew was sitting right next to the front door) and ship them to me. I gave my container garden to my lab team. I knew they'd divide the plants among themselves and take care of them—they'd always admired my garden.

My life is in transition right now and I don't know exactly where it will take me. I'm living one day at a time. All I know is I'll be here until I turn twenty-one, then I'll no longer legally be Thayne's ward and then I can go anywhere. But who knows where that will be?

As I walk to the greenhouse, I see gardeners are cutting back more flowers than usual today, and the clippings from the blossoms are accumulating in piles of delicate beauty. How can I possibly let this splendor go to waste? I bring out a basket and collect the choicest of all the flowers, pausing to sniff each of them to evaluate the best scent. Then I take them inside the greenhouse with me and put together a few tiny bouquets of fresh cut flowers.

I decide to leave one on Barnabas's desk. He does so much around here and he needs to be recognized. I pick out a gorgeous red flower and another white blossom, as well as sprigs of blue and tie them together with trailing vine. Then I sneak into his office at the manor and settle it on the top of his desk with a handwritten note in the Hyrrokin language on old-fashioned parchment:

Thank you for everything you do.

And then I run away, happy with my anonymous, random act of kindness.

And then I get the great idea to do more of these. Milli deserves one too, doesn't she? And Grimwall, the housekeeper, she needs one. I end up busy with the making of my thank you bouquets. What do I give to the head gardener who already has enough flowers? I make a large bouquet that she can take home to her ailing mother. I then leave one for the chef and one for the porter at the front door. Oooh, and the driver and the pilot and… Okay, that's all I'm able to get done this week before the rainy season starts. But eventually, I'll make sure I get around to having made one for every single staff member—this might take a while, but I'll make sure it happens.

I giggle as I leave one on Thayne's desk.

He's working from the manor today and I've been spying on him from a distance for at least the last thirty minutes. Finally, he steps out for a meeting in the front reception room. Now is my chance! I run inside and leave the bouquet and my note on his enormous antique ebony desk, then I dart back out of his office.

I stay hidden around the corner as he reenters, knowing he will find it. He picks up the bouquet and holds the blossoms to his nose and I watch as he reads the note. Then he looks up in my general direction and I push back from my hiding spot and rush off down the hall. Oh shoot, he almost caught me. The whole fun in this is it being a secret gift. They must not know who is leaving these gifts! Well, they might guess it's me, but they don't know for certain.

That evening at dinner Thayne mentions that secret bouquets are being left behind by an anonymous gifter and I pretend to try and figure out who this being can be. It's too much fun.

Afterwards we walk together to his office where he gets back to work at his desk. And I bring my tablet along and sit in yet another comfortable chair in front of another enormous stone fireplace, crackling with a comforting fire. Sometimes I'm focusing on my studies while he works, but often I'm secretly sending silly messages to either Rebyka or Ariana. It's fun.

Ariana and I like to send each other pictures of our "men" caught looking handsome when they don't even know. It might seem weird of me to join in on this considering Thayne isn't "mine," but I can't help it. He's just that good-looking.

Last night I sent Ariana a covert pic of Thayne's veiny forearm, resting on his desk. Ariana sent back a swoon emoji. Then in return she sent me a pic of a ferocious Skoll Strikestone, asleep on their couch with two large kittens snuggled on his chest.

Okay, you win, I responded.

Ariana kept one-upping me so much with those kitten pics I had to tell her she's not allowed to use kittens anymore. The next day she sent pics of Skoll cooking for her, which is also really good.

But then I sent a pic of Thayne looking out his office window with a brooding expression, with one claw braced above his head on the window frame, and we agree it deserves that day's grand prize.

Today I got Rebyka to play along with us. I sent yet another pic of Thayne looking studious. Ariana sends a pic of Skoll polishing a sword. But Rebyka trumps us all when she sends a pic of her female, in a field of blossoms, having just picked a flower and handing it to her. The female's eyes are so full of love for Rebyka, I instantly tear up at the beauty.

Damn, you win today. Both Ariana and I respond almost in unison. *That's true love.*

I WAKE UP ON SATURDAY, excited. I've been at the manor for a week now and today is my birthday.

But it seems like no one remembers.

I'm trying not to get weepy over it, but…I'm sad. It's not like I kept it a secret. I've told everyone, many times, that today is my birthday. I'm not the type who expects everyone to go through any kind of elaborate celebration, but since I kept prompting them, you'd think that at the very least Milli would remember to say a quick "happy birthday" this morning. But nope, she's been totally silent.

Thayne hasn't even messaged me about it. Even Ariana and Rebyka are silent today. And no one in the greenhouse acts like they know today is any different for me from any other day.

Yesterday I left a Happy Birthday bouquet I handmade for the head porter on his desk in the employee break room for his birthday and we had a whole discussion about how the very next day was my birthday—and today I went right past him as he opened the front door for me and…not a word about it from him.

Ouch.

I'm trying to not let everyone's silence hurt my feelings. Maybe Ariana is busy with work today and…maybe birthdays aren't important to Hyrrokin like they are to humans?

It's the afternoon now and I go into the employee wing because Barnabas sent me a message asking me to come and speak to him about my Hyrrokin classes. I guess he wants to check on my progress? I'm smiling because it's like I'm meeting up with one of my professors from back home.

The butler's office is behind the kitchen. I hear voices and open a door and that's when I discover that actually this isn't just one small office for Barnabas, but an entire series of offices, full of staff. Wow. No wonder Barnabas is able to get so much done for Thayne.

Barnabas steps out to greet me and he gives me a warm smile. I've noticed that in just the last day or two he's coming around a bit.

I look around. "I always wondered how you managed to do so much. Now I know."

He nods in agreement. "My line has served the Ashmoors for centuries. Come with me, Lady Ashmoor, there is something I must show you."

I blink with surprise. "Oh, okay."

And then he guides me out of the offices and down a hallway and back into the dark kitchen "What…?"

And then lights flick on and a huge chorus of deep Hyrrokin voices yells out, "Surprise!"

"Aaaah!" I scream with delight.

Oh wow, a surprise birthday party for me?

When has anyone done this for me? Never.

And everyone is here, including Ariana. That sneak! Basically, it's a roll call of all the beings I shook hands with when I arrived here a week ago, along with my human friend. Ariana rushes forward to give me a tight hug and hand over another gift basket, this one is so heavy I have to immediately set it on the table.

My tablet flares to life with a large, flashy Happy Birthday message from Rebyka.

Milli hugs me close. "Do you like the party?" she eagerly questions. "Oh my gosh, it was so hard not saying anything to you this morning. But I didn't want to mess up the surprise. I made the decorations and Grimwall picked out the blossoms. Chef even made special human treats."

"Yes, yes, of course I do, thank you so much."

I look over Milli's shoulder while we talk, and I meet the dark gaze of the fire lord. He's leaning back with his arms crossed and one bare foot braced against the wall. Thayne's here too? I can't believe they all managed to hide this from me.

It turns out they were sweet and they researched human birthday parties, so there is no flame-throwing, which makes me happy. The flames on the candles of my cake are enough to burn a house down and there is no way I can blow them out myself. And right then Thayne steps up to blow them out for me.

"I alone will blow out her flames," he announces to the staff with his impossibly deep voice. "Only I and no one else."

They all nod in agreement. I'm not sure what that whole exchange means but it seems important to everyone else.

"I'm twenty years old now," I remind Thayne as we stand together, eating blood cake. "I'm legal." I wish he was the groom who'd been standing at the altar in front of me back on New Earth. But I know he's kept me at a distance because he thought I was too young for him. Well, that's not the only reason, but one obstacle at a time.

His voice deepens. "I know, female. But the fact still remains that I'm never taking another bound." And then he puts down his plate and walks away, just like he did that night he kissed me.

I blow out a breath.

He warned me he has trust issues due to the death of his former bound and the loss of his son. I need to give him space, but it's so hard when we live together, and his room is right next to mine.

So. Very. Hard.

15

THAYNE

The suns have set and I'm in my office with the door locked, drinking enough fire-alcohol for five large Hyrrokin. Rain pours outside like a stampede of fire-beasts. The rainy season has begun with its usual animosity. Lightning strikes the ground, leaving depressions and burn marks, accompanied by the echoing boom of thunder. I ignore it all and lean back in my chair and pour myself another finger of amber liquid.

I cancelled dinner with my ward again tonight. I've been deliberately avoiding her, and everyone else, since her surprise birthday party. My mood grows darker and darker as the hours edge toward the anniversary of the diurnal when it all happened —the day and time my son was murdered by his own mother.

I take out the letter that Letecia left behind for me as explanation for her actions on the day she decided to kill herself and my son, in a blaze of fire at the estate's multigod temple. I found this message, written on her personal parchment, left on my desk when I returned after my boy's body had been removed for preparation for the afterlife by the morticians. I've kept this letter close ever since, ready to reread whenever I start to forget.

Because I can *never* forget.

I woke up early that day, three years ago, and went directly to Wylik's room to tickle and kiss by beautiful boy, loving his sweet scent and the dark puffs of Ashmoor smoke that escaped his nostrils when he laughed. His nanny was ready with a new schedule for the coming rainy season that would include indoor entertainment and education.

I took his hand and walked him downstairs for breakfast with me and his grandmother. Wylik adored his grandmother and ran to meet her for kisses and a tight hug. My mother put Wylik right next to her and fed him by claw. My son was the center of my mother's world; the two were very close. After breakfast, the Dowager left with my son and the nanny to play together in the gardens, trying to squeeze in the last bit of the sunlight before the seasonal rains.

That afternoon, everyone thought Wylik was napping. His nanny was downstairs, on her scheduled break. My mother was gone, meeting with friends for a late luncheon. I was in my suite, changing my clothes and reading correspondence. I had no idea as to the whereabouts of my bound, but then I never did. She'd grown more and more distant and reserved in the previous months.

Then I saw through my window, over the hills, a single flame and a trail of smoke. The multigod temple, built in the fire age, the oldest building on the estate, older than the manor—was on fire. I learned later that Letecia had used an accelerant to heighten the flames.

By the time I arrived with the fire-banking team, we were only able to blow out a small portion of the flames, then we had to resort to water hosing. The fire was out of control, and we all kept at a distance because it was an empty building. The nanny arrived, screaming and crying, pointing at the burning building. "Lord Ashmoor, Lord Ashmoor...your bound, Lady Ashmoor t... took Lord Wylik...she took him to the *temple!*"

I roared with rage and barreled inside, past the raging fire and the collapsing ceiling and walls, searching again and again for Wylik. Burning beams hit my back and seared my neck and I ignored the pain and kept looking for my son, hoping to find him alive. Finally, I bent down and found the charred remains of my small son, underneath the front seats in the temple.

I was too late. He was dead.

My son had been hiding, trying to save himself. I carefully lifted his scorched and mutilated body and carried it in my arms outside of the burning temple and all the way back to the manor, tears streaming down my face. I remember my mother arriving on the scene, screaming for Wylik, but I continued walking.

I sat down on the front steps of the manor, with my dead boy in my arms, weeping. Hours later they were finally able to pry him away from me so he could be seen by the attending Doctor to officially pronounce time of death.

I never personally checked for Letecia's body. I learned later she died too, and she had set the blaze. She'd swallowed poison and made our son swallow some too and they both died instantly as the flames overtook them. I went into the office afterwards, after I'd left my son's body, dirty from the smoke, ignoring the pain of the burns on my own body, and found her note.

I stoically read the words she'd left behind for me, explaining her reasons for what she'd done. And then I stayed in the office, my room, or Wylik's nursery, mainly alone, for the next moon cycle. I ignored the running of the Ashmoor corporation and everyone who tried to console me. My mother could not coax me out of my depression, nor could my brother. There were many times I thought of ending my own life, but my responsibilities as fire lord kept nagging at the back of my mind.

One day my mother arrived in my room, weeping, and would not leave. She begged me to return to the land of the living. She'd lost her husband and her grandson, and she needed her older son. The words finally penetrated, and I used the cleansing unit, ate some food and began checking my messages again. I slowly rejoined the world. But I've never been the same.

And now my mother is gone too. Only Bane and I remain of our former family. If I had done things different, Wylik would still be with us.

I lift the parchment and reread Letecia's dark words, committing them to memory. Wylik has been gone for three years—if he had lived, he would be six years old now. Each year I read Letecia's words, relive the harrowing memories and remind myself why I can't have another bound. Why I can't be trusted to have another child in my care. I was not able to save Wylik. I do not deserve another child.

I take another drink and gaze pensively at the fire. Then I snarl and toss my bottle into the fireplace, not caring about the loud crash or the spray of broken shards that wake the staff. Not caring about anything.

How can Charlotte possibly want me?

I'm not good for any female.

THAT NIGHT I lie in bed and have a dream more real than any I've experienced in my life.

A flash of lightning and the sound of pounding rain enter my consciousness. A boom of thunder rattles the windows.

Then I hear a distant shriek and Charlotte races through the connecting door. She leaps onto my bed and burrows under the covers with me. "Oh, my gods, you're naked," she exclaims.

In my dream I smile because she's wearing very little clothing. Her legs brush against my hard cock and I lose my mind. All I know is that Charlotte is here, with me and I want her desperately. In my dream actions move quickly and I take her in my arms. In moments she's underneath me and I have my hips between her open thighs and my tongue in her mouth. I've never been this enflamed in my entire life.

She breaks free of my lips and cups my face with her tiny hands "Thayne…are you sure? Is this what you want?"

I growl in agreement because of course this is what I want. In real life I can't have her, but in my dreams I'm able to hold my human in my arms, touch and lick every part of her delectable body and sink inside of her, without worrying about consequences.

I pound out my frustrations, my emotions, I give her all of me. I fuck her all night long with the passion I've been holding inside since the moment we met.

It's the best dream of my life.

THE NEXT MORNING I awake to the sound of rain hammering outside the windows. I suffer from a raging headache, dry mouth and…and my arms are around a naked female.

What? We're both naked and the bedding smells of sex.

Lots and lots of sex.

Human eyes blink open and gaze up at me. This female has no tail, horns or claws. Her skin is colorless, she's… "Charlotte?" I rasp.

My ward stretches lazily and gives me a sexy, satisfied smile. "Good morning sweetheart."

I leap out of bed.

She sits up, startled. "What are you doing? What's wrong?" Her breasts are bare and her large nipples look raw and red and begging to be sucked, again. My shaft is hard and leaking, ready to slide back to its new home between her thighs. She looks down at my red cock and licks her lips.

I took advantage of this female and used her to satisfy my lust? I throw my head back and let out a roar of rage.

I march over to the dresser and take out dark pajama bottoms and pull them on. I turn back to Charlotte and see a look of worry cross her smooth features. The sheet is over her chest, but a single shapely leg is still bare. She looks like a female who was thoroughly fucked last night. By me.

I thought I was dreaming; I didn't know it was real. But I should've known. Anger at myself and the situation in general rushes through my veins. "What are you doing here?" I growl.

She sucks in a sharp breath. Then she stands up, pulling the sheets off the bed with her as she goes. "I was afraid of the storm last night and I ran in here."

"You came into my room without permission?"

She whimpers. "I...I was afraid. And you're the one who placed us next door to each other, with a connecting door you keep unlocked!"

I hang my head, shame replacing my earlier rage. She is right, I was asking for a mistake such as this to occur. "I am sorry I took advantage of you. This was a mistake, and it is all my fault."

"A mistake?" she chokes.

I immediately want to take back that phrasing, but it's already out there.

"A mistake?" she repeats. "You think what we did last night was a mistake?

"I can barely remember it," I admit. "What did we do? I assume we pleasure mated."

Tears form in her eyes. "That was the best night of my life, and you can barely remember it?"

I step forward, ready to pull her into my embrace and comfort her, but she steps back. "Don't touch me," she hisses. "I was the one who came in here without permission, so this was really all my fault. I'm the one who is sorry. I'll leave."

"No, this isn't your fault. I took advantage of you."

"Thayne, you didn't take advantage of me. I'm an adult. I came into your room because I was scared of the storm and then I found you naked in bed and you pulled me into your arms and kissed me and well, it escalated from there. But I stopped to ask you if this was what you wanted and you said yes. I thought there was mutual consent, but I guess I was wrong."

"I was drinking and not myself," I explain hoarsely through my raging headache. "I drank many bottles of fire-alcohol last night. When I found you in my bed, I thought I was dreaming."

"You were drunk? Oh no," she groans. "I tasted alcohol on you, but I thought it was from that one drink you usually have after dinner. I didn't know. I'm so very sorry."

"No, I'm sorry. I told you that we could not mate and then I took you. This is my fault."

"I made sure to ask first if you were sure about us having unprotected sex because you'd been so adamant this wasn't going to happen…But I didn't know you were drunk so your answer wasn't clear-headed." She stands with the sheet wrapped around her middle, tears welling in her expressive eyes. "What are we going to do now?"

I cannot believe I filled this female with my seed. I cannot have more offspring. I cannot. But now the time for choice might be past. I've locked myself into a course of action I did not want. "I pleasure mated you last night and I didn't use birth control," I growl. "We will wait and see if you are pregnant. Meanwhile, we will revert to our normal guardian and ward roles."

Her eyes flash with anger. "You're saying you regret having sex with me and don't want to be with me, or touch me again and you're waiting on seeing if I'm pregnant so you can then decide whether I should keep my baby or not?"

"We will keep the baby!" I thunder.

"Okay then, at least we agree on something."

And then she stomps over to the connecting door, opens it and walks through to her own room and slams the door shut behind her, and locks it for good measure.

. . .

THE NEXT DAY I step out of my office and run into my pregnant female.

Charlotte does not yet know she carries my offspring, but I know because this morning her pheromones shifted from one scent trail into two distinct and separate trails.

And now I am more confused than ever.

She tries to sweep past me and head for the front door, but I grab her delicate hand in mine and pull her close. She's dressed in rain gear, but I can still clearly see the curve of her breasts, the nip of her waist and that ass. I want nothing more than the ability to drag her into my office and push her over my desk, pull down her pants and fuck her from behind.

Memories of our night of highly erotic pleasure mating are beginning to return with startling clarity.

"Where are you going?" I growl.

"Oh, I'm about to go on a tour of the grounds of the estate. I was told there is so much more to see beyond the manor and the formal gardens so I—"

"Who is taking you on this tour?" Rage boils inside of me at the thought of someone, other than me, explaining the history of this land to her.

She takes a step back. "Th….the Head Gardener's assistant?"

My jaw clenches. "Hortwall? The male assistant who is presently unmated?"

"Yes," she answers brightly, doing a good job of pretending we are back to our normal roles of guardian and ward. "He offered to take me. Isn't that nice of him?"

"I am taking you out on this tour, not him."

She glances at the front door which a porter has now opened. I'm certain she has a direct view of Hortwall, the second most eligible bachelor in the county, dressed in similar rain gear, standing at attention on the cobblestone driveway next to an all-terrain vehicle. "B…but he's standing in the rain, waiting for me…"

I could care less. Hortwall can wait for another female, not mine. "I am taking you on this tour of the estate," I repeat.

"Aren't you busy with work?"

"Barnabas!" I shout.

"Yes sire?"

"Cancel my meeting, I am instead taking Lady Ashmoor on a tour of the estate. Order the Chef to pack us a picnic—"

She places a palm on my forearm. "Oh, Thayne don't worry about that. I think Hortwall already has a picnic packed for us to eat when we reach the hunter's lodge…"

Smoke wafts from my nostrils. I look over at Barnabas. "Make sure nothing like this ever happens again. Understood?"

"Yes, sire. I will alert the staff."

"Make sure *what* never happens again?"

I put on the rain gear Barnabas offers me, then I take Charlotte's hand in mine and lead her outside and down the steps to the all-terrain vehicle. Hortwall has smartly decided to make himself scarce.

We drive out through the brief respite, between the heavy storms. The skies are still dark, but the rain is gentle, and I have the headlights on to show us the way. She points at the shadowy outline of an ancient grey stone building built into the slope of a hill. "Can we stop there and go inside and look at that? What is it?"

"This is the Ashmoor family mausoleum." I park next to the gate, my fingers tightening on the steering wheel.

"Oh."

"Targek Ashmoor has recently been interred here. I made sure his remains were transferred from New Earth to Tarvos so he can be inside the Ashmoor mausoleum, where he belongs."

"Oh really? Can I see? I'd love to have the ability to pay my respects."

It's a reasonable request so I force myself to step out of the vehicle and walk up to the front door. The vault is dusty, and I blow flames to ignite the torches and wall scones. I haven't been inside the mausoleum since the day my mother was interred.

I see the name plagues for my mother and my son and the empty spaces on either side of them. My gaze hardens and my jaw ticks. I refused to have my former bound's remains placed here. She is interred at her own family's mausoleum, on the other side of the planet.

"Thayne, what's wrong?" my female innocently questions.

I can't do this anymore. "I will wait for you outside," I respond hoarsely and step back out to the vehicle.

16

CHARLOTTE

I feel terrible that I led Thayne into the mausoleum. I'm a human who thinks this vault is a curious historical building, with no personal meaning to me, but he said my grandfather had been placed there so I wanted to go inside and see. The plaques for the placement of his mother and his son are what Thayne sees first and he looks upset.

How insensitive can I be? I can easily come back another time.

Of course his mother and son would be there, and his father, as well as all his family going back a thousand years. I went outside with tears in my eyes, begging his forgiveness.

He was very gracious about the whole thing and swore he was fine. "We will return another time, together," he says. And then he insisted we continue our rainy tour of the other outbuildings on the estate and that we eat lunch together in the rustic hunter's lodge.

Somehow we managed to have a nice time, despite the fact that we were both pretending we hadn't had sex and Thayne hadn't called it a "mistake."

I cannot believe I had hot, intimate sex with my guardian,

Lord Ashmoor, only for it to be taken away. I was given the best treat in the world and now it's gone. And the entire time we were in the lodge I was desperately wishing he'd strip me naked and take me again on the rug in front of the crackling fire. Because even if he doesn't remember what happened, I do. And I want more.

Today I stare out the window of the dowager's suite at the driving rain and it makes me sad because I loved going for walks in the gardens in the sparkly sunshine. Everyone tried to warn me that it would rain every single day for a whole damn month. And not sprinkles, but unrelenting downpour along with occasional scary thunderstorms.

I'm solar powered, so now that the sun is gone and replaced with nothing but dark gray skies both day and night, I feel depressed. Although I'm not certain if it's due to the weather or the fact that Thayne basically kicked me out of his bed yesterday morning, after he'd discovered he'd accidentally had drunken sex with me.

I take another sip of Traq and try not to cry again, and instead concentrate on the weather.

I guess I didn't think the rains would be this bad, because how could I understand? I was born and raised on New Earth which is semi-arid. Summertime on Tarvos is when it rains the hardest? On my home planet it rains for only six months, during the coldest part of the year. The rest of the time it rains little and in the summer it almost never rains. Rain in the summertime is completely foreign to me. Hurricanes and flash floods happen on other planets, not on New Earth. A whole moon cycle of driving rain and dark days is so strange to me. But they are used to it here, there's a whole lake on the edge of the estate that is filling up with nothing but rainwater runoff.

The lightning, thunder and wailing wind began and I wasn't prepared for it. I seriously think thunder is louder here on this planet.

Maybe I should've left the curtains closed so I could sleep, but I had to open them; I needed to see what was happening. I freaked out at the wind whipping the trees and how, even though I knew the staff had tied everything down, I could still see objects snapping free and flying through the air.

A flash of lightning hit the ground just outside my window and the thunder cracked so loud it reverberated in my chest. And that was when I let out a shriek and ran through the connecting door, because I thought the manor was about to be destroyed by the storm.

I flew into Thayne's room and went to his bed. His curtains were also open, and the fireplace glowed so I could see his outline; somehow sleeping through the raging storm I thought was about to destroy us all.

Tears streamed down my face.

The room lit with another flash of lightning and an even scarier boom of thunder. "Thayne!" I hit the bed and crawled straight for him. I can't help it, I love him, and I was scared, so I head for Thayne.

Maybe the problem was that I was wearing only a tiny Hyrrokin cropped tube top and a pair of barely-there undies? It was a warm, sultry evening, so I was dressed light. And after I got my arms around him, I quickly realized he was naked and aroused.

Uh oh.

I tried to scoot away, realizing my mistake, but he growled and his arms went around me and his lips devoured mine. And things escalated quickly.

Okay, maybe I needed something to keep my mind off the storm? And wow, it certainly did. But now I feel like a bitch who used him for mind-blowing sex. I knew I wasn't on birth control. I was the one who snuck into his bed and latched onto him. I was scared, but still, I could've kept my hands to myself. I'm an adult who knew when he slid that massive cock inside of me and started coming, what that could mean and in the back of my mind I decided to take that risk.

In my defense I did pause, right after he rolled on top of me and placed his cock at my wet entrance and I asked him if he was sure. He'd told me time and time again, very clearly that he did not want to have a bound or more offspring. And we both know I don't want to only be his pleasure mate.

I was fully ready to keep my legs closed. I could've switched to sucking him off instead, no problem. But he said he wanted this, so I was all "carry on."

Godsdammit. How was I to know he wasn't able to fully give his clear consent because he was drunk? He'd always seemed so in charge and sure of himself, so I took his words at face value.

I knew he didn't want to get married or have more children. But since I didn't know he was drunk I thought he was taking a chance like I was, knowing in the end the outcome wouldn't be upsetting. Maybe I thought he was swept away by it all and he'd realize his love for me in that bed? I thought I'd wake up to a proposal. I mean, I was ready to propose to *him* the next morning. And instead, I woke up to a male who was horrified to discover he'd had drunken, unprotected sex with me.

I didn't know he'd been so distraught over his past that he'd drank himself into a stupor. I had no idea that last night was the anniversary of the death of his child, which apparently is a day he routinely spends drunk and in his office in a terrible mood. The weather I'm sure never helps. It must be as if the entire planet is crying too.

I didn't see him at all that day. I thought he was out on a business trip to the main city. I did try and message him and he didn't respond, but this wasn't completely unusual, so I wasn't concerned yet.

The staff was hiding his behavior from me. They were probably used to protecting him in this way. They give him space, let him mourn, and then they help him sober up and move on.

And Thayne thinks he's the one who used me? It's crazy. If anyone is at fault here it is me for not asking him more than once, or just flat out saying no and making us wait until the next morning. I got swept away by my desire for that sexy Hyrrokin.

But I'm not some idiot. I'm a girl who knows what she wants. I wanted Thayne and I thought he wanted me too. I knew the risks because I wasn't on birth control. And now I might be pregnant.

I stare down at my stomach.

What if I *am* pregnant?

That would be perfectly fine with me. I love the idea of starting a family. Lots of young women back on New Earth were determined to wait at least a decade before having children, if at all. But I'd always liked the idea of having a large family. It was always a secret dream of mine.

I refuse to think of this as a mistake. It was the best night of my life. If that was Thayne while drunk, I cannot imagine what sex with him must be like when he is perfectly sober and paying complete attention to the task.

I let out a dreamy sigh and sip more of my Traq.

THREE WEEKS later I rush to the bathroom and throw up.

Oh hells, I'm pregnant. That was quick! It was nice thinking about it, but now it's reality. Jeez, Thayne is incredibly virile. We only had sex that one time. Oh wait, actually we had sex over and over again that one night. So, yeah maybe it was more possible than I'd thought. I'm going to have to tell him. And then he'll drag me down to the med lab and confirm it. And...

"You're pregnant."

I sit up, startled. Thayne is standing behind me, in the bathroom. He's never once been in this suite since I've arrived, let alone the bathroom. And now he arrives? I reach up and flush the toilet. And then the sickness rushes up again and I'm gagging and throwing up a second time.

Ugh.

He sits behind me, touching me on the waist and shoulder and hands me a wet wipe for my mouth. I start to cry because I can't help it and he's holding me in his arms. I'm pregnant by a Hyrrokin who doesn't even want to marry me or have a baby. I'm going to be a single mother. This isn't how I meant for this to play out.

"You're mine now."

I push him away and glare at the man who doesn't want me. "*Now* you want me? Thayne, you've been avoiding me for the last three weeks. You took me on that tour of the outbuildings and that was it. You don't have dinner with me anymore and you don't let me into your office at night."

He pulls me back into his arms and I go right back because he smells so good. "Charlotte, I messaged you three times each diurnal. We've chatted each and every day. I've watched your every movement. How do you think I know you're in here?"

"But I haven't *seen* you," I whine. "So, I'm surprised that you're finally showing up."

"Female, I needed to keep my distance so I didn't try to pleasure mate you again. But now that we *both* know you are carrying my offspring, this changes everything. When you give birth to my heir you will automatically become my bound."

I should be happy at this pronouncement but it's a stab in the heart. "You only want me because I'm carrying your baby. You don't want *me*."

"You are mine."

"I don't have to be your bound for you to be a father. We can live separate lives in entirely different domiciles and you can see your baby constantly," I say, trying to give him a way out. I love him, but I don't know if he can ever truly love me in return.

Midnight black smoke wafts from his nostrils. "You are *mine*," he repeats.

THAT NIGHT the connecting door suddenly unlocks. I sit up in my bed and pull the covers up to my chest. Thayne arrogantly stands in the doorway, in nothing but a pair of dark pajama pants, looking as grim and luscious as he did that night I jumped into his bed and thrust my tongue in his mouth.

He crosses his massive red arms and says with a voice that could grind rocks, "You will have dinner again with me each evening and afterwards you will return with me to my office and…you will also start sleeping with me each night in my bed."

My nostrils flare. "Now that I'm pregnant with your child I'm suddenly worthy?"

He doesn't bother to respond. He just marches over and scoops me out of my bed and carries me in his arms back through the connecting door and drops me onto his own bed.

Oh!

The worst part is I don't even try to get up. I huff out an agitated breath, punch a pillow into the position I want and roll onto my side, facing away from him. But I stay right where he puts me.

The bed dips and a huge, virile Hyrrokin male lies down behind me. Butterflies instantly take flight in my belly. He wraps a red forearm around my thick middle and pulls me back against his huge, warm body. And I can't hide a tiny sigh of delight. I feel small and delicate in his embrace.

That hard shaft prods my ass and my clit throbs for his attention. I'm wetter than wet because I fantasize that I can lift a leg and he'll slide that enormous red cock right inside of me, filling me up again as he did the night of the storm. And then he'll grab my ass and knead it as he plows in and out.

He has no idea how much I miss his cock.

That first moment when it bottoms out. The movement back and forth. It's large and smooth and taste's great. I spent a long time licking and sucking on his balls while lightning flashed outside. They're basically my favorite feature of his.

Thayne shoves his face into my hair and inhales. His muscles relax and his chest rises and falls with even breaths. "As my offspring grows inside of you," he rumbles, "so does the scent of your pheromones. I now need both scent trails next to me in order to sleep."

I bite my lip but don't answer. I just shift my legs, trying to find relief for the aching, empty place between my thighs. I'm wearing a short nightgown and no underwear whatsoever because I've always secretly wanted back in his bed. I'm angry at him and yet I want him so badly. I'm a mess.

He places a hand on my hip. "I will tend to you, female."

I know he can smell my arousal, so I don't even try and pretend I don't know what he's talking about. "You will? For reals?"

"This is why you are always angry with me?"

"Mainly," I admit. "It's hard for me to think straight with so many hormones rushing through me. We had sex before and I remember it very clearly and I miss it. I want more. And now I'm in your bed and your erection is pressed against my ass. I can't handle it. And I resent you for putting me in this situation without giving me relief."

"I understand."

His claw cups my ass and his chest rumbles. "I love your ass," he breathes against my ear. He spends time caressing my buttocks and then he lifts my leg. I rest it back onto one of his calves, allowing a bit more room for him to access the space between my thighs. His claw-tipped fingers dip into me from behind, inside my channel. We both let out long groans of delight.

"You're so wet," he rasps.

"For you," I tell him. "I've never been this wet before."

"This is how you were that night."

"You remember?"

His tongue trails along my shoulder. "I remember everything. The erotic follicles on the lips of your cunt, your thick thighs and your perfect ass." And then he spends time thrusting his fingers inside of me, careful of his claws. I shudder when a finger rubs perfectly on my clit.

"Pinch your nipples," he orders.

Damn, I love it when he gives me orders. I do as he says and the climax rushes in swift and urgent. I hold onto the tip of his tail as I scream with the force of the orgasm.

He lets go of me and pulls down the edge of my nightgown and covers the both of us with the bedding.

"But…" I comment, reaching back to grope for his erection.

"No, we will not go further. I will tend to your needs each morning and every evening, here in our bed. That is all."

I'm sad because I really wanted to watch and feel him come. "You're going to deny yourself? Isn't that…uncomfortable?"

He growls and then pulls me back into his arms.

"I don't understand you," I whisper into the darkness. "You run hot and cold, and I can't keep up."

"This is fine. I often don't understand myself either," he admits.

And then I close my eyes and fall asleep.

EACH MORNING I rush out of Thayne's bed to throw up. I've never vomited this much in my entire life.

My sexy fire lord always wakes long before I do and goes down to the basement where he keeps a scary-looking workout room filled with heavy-duty exercise equipment specifically built for sweaty, fire-breathing Hyrrokin males. This is why he gets up so early!

HIS HUMAN WARD

Milli meets me in the bathroom, checking in and offering words of comfort and encouragement as well as a fortifying mug of Traq afterwards, which is so nice of her. After my stomach settles, I clean and dress for the day.

I pad downstairs into the quiet kitchen. The head chef is already there, starting the bread for the day and it always smells so good. "Good morning," I say brightly because I'm a morning person. Chef grins back at me and points at the counter space next to him that he readies for me.

I like arriving here early so I can get the first fire-scones out of the oven. They always settle my stomach. It's basically the only food I'm able to keep down lately.

I've come to realize this kitchen, the offices and the nearby workrooms are the center of the Ashmoor fandom and the staff here are super fans. And I've joined their fandom without reservation. Who knew I'd love it so much? Certainly not me. The moment I left New Earth for Tarvos, I was charmed. Well, really the moment Thayne swept me off my feet and carried me from that Church, I was charmed.

I am a citizen of Tarvos, set to inherit an ancient Ashmoor title, and now I'm also carrying a half-Hyrrokin, half-human baby. I truly understand now, how Targek Ashmoor could've been so in love with my grandmother that he left his home planet to happily live the rest of his life with her on New Earth.

I sprinkle flour on the dough. Meanwhile negative thoughts enter my mind again: Maybe Thayne doesn't truly want me. He wants this baby, which is sweet. He said before that he didn't want more offspring, but each night he tenderly cups my pregnant belly in his huge claw while he sleeps. Those are not the actions of a male who doesn't want another child. But does he really want me? It's just the law of this planet that is forcing him to keep me. And his addiction to my pregnancy pheromones.

I clear my throat and take another sip of Traq.

Chef lets me quietly knead dough with him and then while it

proofs, we sip tasty, infused hot water he pours over a glass kettle filled with gorgeous herbs and blossoms he picked from the estate garden. The yellow and pink blossoms along with the deep green herbs are fascinating to watch as they shrink in the hot water. The steeped, herb-infused water is basically better than Traq, if that's possible. Watching a black-horned male as ferocious as the Head Chef, delicately lift and sip from his mug is a study in opposites.

Then we bake the batch we have, while making more dough for the second batch. The work clears my head and allows me to think of Thayne instead of myself.

Thayne's heartache over the loss of his child is still fresh in his mind, as if it happened yesterday. I want to help him grab onto future happiness, but I don't know how. And I'm ninety-nine percent certain he won't see a grief counselor because he thinks he's a big strong male who doesn't need this kind of help, even though he does.

But when he found out I was pregnant with his child he demanded I sleep in the same bed with him each night. I guess having me next door, with a connecting door wasn't good enough. I want more than his fingers and tongue. I want to be able to touch him too and have him inside of me. I'm pregnant and horny and I need his cock.

I pound my fist into the dough, taking my frustrations out on the gluten.

I suppose we both have trust issues. I was recently traumatized by a fake groom, best friend and mother-in-law, who were all faking their feelings for me so they could steal currency from me. And Thayne had it much, much worse, his ex-wife and son died in a fire. Pain flairs again in my chest over his loss. How does a parent ever move past the violent death of a child?

Grimwall enters the kitchen to munch on some of the scones coming out of the oven and starts flirting with Chef, also a widower. She thinks I don't notice, but of course I do. They're both widowers and this is half the fun showing up here each morning, watching these two older Hyrrokin who've both lost their bounds, act like they aren't secretly pleasure mating.

The three of us end up chatting.

"The manor used to be full of life and laughter, but now it isn't." Grimwall says with a wistful tone. "There have been many losses, many family members sadly passing away, so the fire lord has been in mourning for several years now. He's began having the required functions each season, but no one stays the night. There are rarely any guests. It is very quiet here."

"Too quiet," the Chef agrees.

"This is a manor meant to be filled with Ashmoors."

And then they both turn to stare at me, and I shift uncomfortably in my seat.

I feel bad for the staff at the manor. Thayne isn't the only one in mourning. Everyone who worked here loved the dowager and Wylik and miss both of them desperately. It makes me want to cry. And I see echoes of Thayne's mother and son everywhere in this mansion. I'm beginning to feel like I knew them. I sleep in the dowager's suite, and I pass by Wylik's old room every day.

"Can you please tell me the entire story of what happened when Wylik passed away?" I ask. "I want to help Lord Ashmoor move past his heartache, but I can't do that if I don't know the whole story. I read a brief summary in the ancestry of what happened, but it didn't say much beyond the facts. And…and Lord Ashmoor won't really speak of it."

Grimwall and Chef exchange loaded glances and then Grimwall nods. She holds my hand in hers and tells me everything, the entire story of Letecia Limestone's suicide and Wylik's eventual death in the great fire. I learn how Letecia poisoned her own son and dragged him into the fire she'd set. And I cry at the image of Thayne, weeping, holding his dead son in his arms on the front steps.

"I think everyone was traumatized by how the boy died. The

nanny was inconsolable. Lady Ashmoor decided to commit suicide by burning down the chapel she'd performed her declaration ceremony in and killed herself and her son in the process. The thought of a small child dying that way, knowing his own mother was the instigator and not his savior—I can barely stand it and I'm not even his actual parent," Grimwall concludes.

Wow.

Later that morning I put on my rain gear and go for a long walk. The rainy season is almost over and today there's a faint glimmer of sunlight and only a lingering drizzle. My mind is full of how I'm almost two months pregnant and here to stay and all that means for my future. And I keep thinking of Thayne and three-year-old Wylik.

I take a road I've never traversed before, beyond the gardens. Over a small rise I find the remains of a burnt out multigod temple. I put my hand over my mouth as I stare at the collapsed stone walls and the rough foundation, tears burning behind my eyes. This is where it happened. Where Thayne lost Wylik.

I walk around the entire site, checking the lay of the land, looking around. And I decide I'm going to have the temple rebuilt. It is time.

I want to be Thayne's bound and the mother of his future offspring and...and I want us to be family. I love him so much.

And right then I decide this man needs me. He needs me to put my hand out and help pull him up.

I want to marry him. I want this man as my bound. But I can't until he's ready to move on and start again. I don't know when that will be, but I almost married the wrong man just a month ago. There's no way I'm going to fall into the wrong marriage again.

I sit down under a tree and take out my tablet and ping Rebyka. She knows what's been happening, I've told her and Ariana both about the disastrous night I took advantage of my drunk guardian and had unprotected sex with him. I used to feel angry at him for denying me more sex and afterwards calling the night we made love a 'mistake', but now I feel angry at myself for putting Thayne in the exact situation he'd told me ahead of time he didn't want to be in.

Rebyka responds right away. *Has he declared for you yet?* she asks.

No. Not yet.

And there it is—this could be proof that Thayne isn't motivated by love. Maybe our relationship is nothing more than a male who knocked up a female he didn't mean to, and he remains close because he's addicted to my pheromones. But then I think of the way he looks at me. How he treats me like a best friend. And he continues to randomly declare "you're mine" at the oddest moments, so I can't help but think we have a future together.

Rebyka tells it like it is: *You're carrying his offspring, so you are his bound. He knows that. Take this time, before the birth of your offspring to open your heart to him and fix what's keeping the two of you apart. Divorce doesn't exist on Tarvos!*

She's so right.

Hyrrokin mate for life.

I've got to plan this out very, very carefully. There's no reason to rush.

17

THAYNE

"Barnabas!"

My butler quickly arrives in my office and gazes out the window beside me.

"What is that about?" I shout, pointing at the caravan of vehicles loaded with supplies making their way over the hills to an area I expressly said was off-limits to all reconstruction. The rainy season is long over and now the roads are dry and passable. This is the best time of the year for projects—I should know because I have plans for many construction projects laid out on my desk.

His lips purse. "I don't know."

A team of workers are traveling up the road I know only leads to the burnt-out temple. There is no reason for this. None. "You don't know?" I sputter. "How is that possible?"

"It shouldn't be possible. I will investi—"

"No," I roar. "I will find out myself what is happening and put a stop to it immediately." Then I throw open my office door and stomp out to the front foyer, without even bothering to put on a sash. I get outside onto the driveway and growl at a passing worker and commandeer his all-terrain vehicle and ride after the group that just disappeared over the hill.

I catch up with them as they are assembling and I'm stunned to find my pregnant female there, with another human I vaguely remember as the bound of Bergelmir Touchstone. They stand conferring, next to the charred remains of the multigod temple. A male who wears a badge from the Hyrrokin Historical Society and who I assume is the architect, is surveying the area and directing a team of workers.

"What the hells is going on here?" I bellow, spittle flying out of my mouth.

I haven't been in this specific location on the estate in years. Not since the night it happened. I'm surprised to see that there's nothing left but the foundation, rows of cracked benches, some stunted stone pillars and one single charred arch.

"Uh oh," I hear Charlotte mutter. "I'll take care this," she tells the others. "Y'all stay here and carry on, I'll talk to him." Then she waves a hand to the beings who invaded my property and calmly walks up to me with a sway of her hips, a smile on her face and a hand placed on the swell of her stomach. "Thayne, I didn't know you'd notice us so quickly. I was really hoping to gift you with this later. It's supposed to be a surprise."

"A surprise?" I sputter. "This is a nightmare." I pull her into my arms and shove my nose into the crook of her neck and inhale. It is the only thing that calms me down.

She places her arms around me and pulls me in tight to her soft embrace and speaks gently against my ear. "Thayne, let me rebuild what was taken from you."

A growl rumbles in my chest. "No."

"Yes." She stands on her toes and kisses me tenderly on the cheek. "Let me do this for you. I promise we'll treat this project with care and respect…and right there," she turns and points, "right there is the spot where we will put a plaque on the wall, dedicating this new temple to Lord Wylik Ashmoor, the beloved son of Thayne Ashmoor, the thirteenth fire lord of Ashmoor. We will always remember him and never forget what he meant to you."

I pull her tighter into my embrace, not wanting the others to see the tears that flood my eyes. "Yes," I croak. "This is acceptable."

ONE HOUR later I'm sitting in my office, in the midst of a security meeting with two imposing soldiers: Skoll Strikestone and Hannibal Hellstone.

I've hired Molten Lava to update the entire security system for the manor. I want my future bound and offspring safe. This is an update I've been meaning to take care of for many years, but now it has become a priority.

My mind wanders, still reliving the shocking moment, earlier today, when I discovered my female was taking on the restoration of the estate's multigod temple. I'm strangely calm at the idea of her taking on such a task, even though I've let no one else consider it until now.

"What do half-Hyrrokin and half-human babies look like?" I question.

Skoll looks up from an old-fashioned paper blueprint of the manor he's been studying. "Heh?" he responds, obviously surprised by this off-topic remark.

"I can answer this," Hannibal cuts in. "So far three half-Hyrrokin, half-human babies have been born on Tarvos and they all appear to have similar markings. They retain tails, claws and horns. And they can flash flame."

I let out a sigh of relief. I will love my offspring no matter what, but the idea of a child who cannot flash-flame makes me sad. I hate the idea of a child not having the ability all Hyrrokin are proudest to inherit.

"I know," Hannibal agrees. "I was relieved too. I was thrilled to hear my daughter's first fire churn in her tiny infant belly and to see a puff of smoke from her delicate nostrils. I know she will be able to defend herself."

"What human characteristics do these bi-species infants retain?"

"They are colorless," Hannibal answers. "None of them keep the Hyrrokin red, but instead have a pigment similiar to the mother. And also, their tail and horns are smaller."

"And not all of them have fangs. Mitry, Hannibal's daughter, doesn't have fangs, her teeth are blunt like a human."

"Yes, there's that," Hannibal agrees. "She has flash-flames but no fangs."

"Why do you ask?" Skoll questions.

I gaze out the window for a moment, and then decide to tell them the truth I haven't even yet told my brother. I turn back around and face them both. "My human ward is pregnant. She is carrying a half-Hyrrokin baby."

Hannibal bursts from his seat, black smoke billowing from both nostrils. "Who has molested your ward? Tell me the name of this scoundrel and I will end him now."

Oh hells.

Skoll continues to stare at me, then shakes his head. "Sit down Hannibal," my neighbor growls, "I think the 'scoundrel' is right here in this room."

"What? Who?"

I lift my chin and say the words that will cause these males to lose all respect for me. "I am the father of her child," I announce. "I pleasure mated with Charlotte and she is carrying my half-human, half-Hyrrokin offspring."

Hannibal sits down heavily. "You? You did this to her?"

I drop my chin. "Yes. Me."

"Was she at least of age when this happened?" Hannibal rages.

Heat races across my cheeks. "Yes. She was of age."

"Barely," Skoll admonishes. "Was their proper consent?"

I clench my fists. "We are in disagreement about this. I say that I did not gain her consent. It happened late at night during the first storm of the rainy season, after I'd drank five bottles of fire-alcohol. She ran into my room because she was frightened. My drunken mind discovered a gorgeous, half-naked female in my bed and took advantage of her. I thought I was dreaming. She says that she took advantage of *me* because she asked for my consent, which I gave, but only because I was drunk and thought I was dreaming. She didn't know I was drunk when she asked for my consent, so she thinks she took advantage of *me*. Neither of us were using birth control. I've kept her away from me after that one night of error. But the moment I discovered she was carrying my offspring, the choice was moot. She is mine."

"After she gives birth to your offspring she will be your bound and the new Fire Marchioness of Ashmoor. And her child will be your heir. Does she know this?"

"She says that she does not want to tie me to my 'mistake' and that I can be a father without formally making her my mate. I think she is considering moving to her own domicile after the birth of our offspring, but she will allow me to see my child whenever I would like."

"She thinks like a human," Skoll snorts. "She doesn't understand she is legally your bound."

"Yes. We recently found out the gender of our offspring. She carries my son. I originally kept her at a distance because she was too young, then because she was my ward and as her guardian it was improper for me to take her as my pleasure mate."

"Improper, but not illegal," Hannibal points out.

"Yes, not illegal. But as the thirteenth Fire Lord of Ashmoor, I refuse to behave in an improper manner. And also...also...there is the matter of my first bound and my oldest son. After their deaths in the great fire of '05 I took a vow that I would never again declare for another bound or have additional offspring. I do not consider myself a fit mate or father."

They both stare at me quizzically.

"But the moment she gives birth, she will be your bound. So isn't this moot? Isn't your vow no longer valid?" Hannibal questions with dispassionate logic.

Skoll turns to gaze at me, waiting for my response to this question.

I have none.

"Have you formally asked her to be your bound in a public ceremony?"

I blow out a breath. "No. She says she will not force me to become her bound when we've only been together the one night, when I was drunk."

"You were just going to wait for the clock to run out and for her to give birth and then she's automatically your bound?"

I shrug.

"That is dishonorable," Skoll remarks.

Fire churns in my chest.

My neighbor leans forward. "I may not like your family, but I've never known your males to leave a female, who was carrying their offspring, without a declaration. If you wait for the clock to run out, she'll never be truly accepted by your snooty aristocracy."

I grimace because it's true.

"They'll consider her less-than because of your lack of respect for her and treat her accordingly. Is this what you want for the mother of your offspring?"

"Let me ask you something," Hannibal cuts in, "do you think pleasure mating this female was a mistake?"

"I...I..."

"Have you ever told her that your one night together was a mistake?"

I swallow. "Yes. I said that. I said it was an error and that I would refrain from touching her again. But I wanted to know if I had impregnated her."

"And then after you found out she was carrying your heir and was going to be your bound, you began wooing her?"

I shift in my seat. "Wooing? What does that mean?"

Hannibal leans forward. "Wooing is a human term, where you spend time with your female. You tell her how much you love her and then you declare for her."

"Love?" I question. Do I love Charlotte Cruz? "Sh...she carries my offspring. I enjoy her company. She treats the staff well..." And if I allowed myself, I could easily fuck her all day long, including nights, weekends and most holidays. And this is exactly why I haven't sunk my cock inside of her again, because I know that's the end of all my protestations. Charlotte isn't simply a pleasure mate to fuck occasionally for our mutual release.

Hannibal throws up his claws. "I can't believe this. You haven't told her how you feel about her, have you? She doesn't know you love her?"

I shake my head. "N...no. I don't lo—"

"Oh, cut it out," Skoll sneers, the scar along the side of his face growing darker. "Remember how disgusted you were when you found out I was intended to another and hadn't yet declared for Ariana? Well, that's how I feel about you right now. You need to get your head out of your ass. You love this human, so you need to treat her with care and respect."

I stare at him in astonishment because I've never been in love. How would I know what it feels like? "I treat my female with care," I protest.

"But not respect," he growls.

"You do love her," Hannibal agrees. "But I can see you're a male who hasn't the faintest idea of love between mates. Let me ask you, Lord Ashmoor, do you think of your female constantly? Is she the first being you consider when you awake and the last being you think of at night?"

"Yes."

"Is her scent so addictive you are unable to sleep unless she is next to you?"

"Yes."

"Does the sound of her voice make your cock hard?"

My voice deepens. "Yes."

"He's got it bad."

"She's your mate."

I lean back in my chair, dumbfounded at these new revelations. "I love Charlotte?"

"Yes, you do. And the way things stand right now she'll think you're only making her your bound because it's the law. The only way you are going to get her to stay in your mansion, happily sleeping in your bed each night with love in her heart, is if you tell her how you feel. You need to Hyrrokin-up and ask her to be your bound in a formal declaration ceremony."

"Fix this," Skoll growls. "And fix it soon."

"Oh my gods," Charlotte exclaims.

"What is wrong?" I question.

We've finished dinner and my pregnant female is sitting in her favorite chair in front of the fireplace in my office with her feet propped up in front of the fireplace. Her tablet rests on her belly. I am working at my desk, trying to document my feelings for her, in preparation for my public statement when I ask her to be my bound. The declaration has to be just right.

This is my favorite time of each diurnal. Later I will take her to bed and lick her between her thighs until she orgasms against my face. Then I'll pull her into my arms and ignore my own throbbing cock. At least I have her in my arms with her scent in my lungs. This is enough for now.

My reasons for refraining from pleasure mating my bound have changed. I now realize I was denying myself as punishment for taking advantage of her in the first place, then because I didn't want to grow closer to her. Because I knew the moment I sank into her I'd know I was home. But now, I'm not afraid of that. I welcome it. I love her. I love Charlotte and I will wait to mate her properly, on the night of our bound declaration ceremony.

"Remember that jerk who I was about to marry on New Earth? The one who was trying to marry me only to steal currency from me, and you carried me away from the wedding?"

"Yes," I growl, "the male I wanted to kill but you forced me to allow him life?"

"Yes, that one. Check this out," she waves her tablet in the air, "he's trying to get on my good side again. He's been messaging me, and I told him in no uncertain terms that I know what he did and I'm never speaking to him or anyone in his family ever again and he's lucky what happened didn't go further so I didn't have to alert the peacekeepers. He didn't actually steal from me, but I think that's mainly because he never had the chance. But he doesn't give up. He keeps messaging me, pointing out that I'm not married yet so he thinks he still has a chance with me. He thinks we can get back together!"

"You are pregnant with my offspring," I growl.

"Right? I told him I'm pregnant and he says he doesn't care, that we can still get back together and he'll raise the baby no matter what species it is. This guy is crazy."

"Tell him that you are taken and that you have a bound."

She gazes at me with bright hazel eyes. "But…but I'm not really taken am I? I won't legally be your bound until I have the baby, and even then, it's just a legality. You said you're never taking another bound, remember?"

Smoke wafts from my nostrils.

She purses her lips and looks back down at her tablet, trying to act like she doesn't care. "It's okay, I'm blocking him," my female says. "This whole thing isn't really a big deal…" and she taps again on her tablet.

And I check my calendar and plan for the best day to gather friends and family in order to propose to my female.

ONE WEEK later Barnabas enters my office and closes the door to make a surprising declaration: "Sire, I need to speak to you, privately."

I crook an eye ridge because this type of behavior from my butler is highly unusual.

"This question comes not just from me, but from the entire staff."

The entire staff? This is even more unusual. And he looks like he needs to speak about something important. The Fire Ball is this evening and Barnabas shuts the door behind him to close out the sounds of chaos in the hallway as the staff readies for tonight's event.

I nod and lean back in my chair, ready to give him my full attention.

He doesn't bother to take a seat but stands in front of my desk and scowls at me. "Why have you not declared yet for Charlotte Cruz?" he demands.

I blink, trying to hide my surprise. "It has been difficult because..." I stand and wander over to the window and rub my claw over my scalp. "Wait, the entire staff wants to know why I am not asking my ward to be my bound?"

"Yes. Your mother, the Dowager, was the social backbone of your family. She was the one who made sure all the family was personally invited to every function. When your former bound chose to not take over that role, your mother kept it up in her stead. But now she is gone. For two years now this manor is empty except for you, the staff and the beings who arrive for your business meetings. This is not the way this grand manor was meant to be run. It is not meant to echo with silence, it should echo with the laughter of family and children. The staff are in agreement. It is nonsensical that Lady Ashmoor is carrying your offspring and sleeps in your bed each night, and yet you have not formally declared for her. Why have you not yet organized a Bound Declaration Ceremony?"

"Because I have not been worthy to declare again," I answer, admitting my deepest shame and regret to the male I spend the most time with in this world. "I have not been able to declare for her or anyone else because of what happened that day in the fire. I vowed to myself that I would never take on another bound ever again, nor would I ever father additional offspring."

A growl rumbles in my butler's chest.

"My former bound killed herself to not only escape me, but to punish me," I remind him, "and I was not able to protect my son. It was my fault that they both died. It was on my watch." I hang my head. "It is my fault that Wylik died."

And then I walk to my desk and open the secret compartment where I keep the letter Letecia left for me on her death. The letter I reread once a year when I hole myself up in here and drink my tears away. I hand it over to Barnabas for him to read. It is the first time I have fully allowed any other being to see the enormity of my shame and dishonor. He takes the parchment in his claws and quietly reads the words that are burned into my memory:

THIS IS ALL YOUR FAULT.

If only you'd loved me at all or loved your son more, I wouldn't have to do this. I hate this place and I hate you most of all. You made me do this, Thayne.

I have to take our son with me into the afterlife.

And now you'll lose everything.

"WHAT IS THIS POISON?" Barnabas snarls. "You've had this in your possession this whole time and never told anyone? No wonder you've had trouble moving past this tragedy." My butler balls the offending parchment up in his fist, steps over to the fireplace and tosses it into the blaze. I watch as the parchment catches fire and the edges burn and the entire paper disintegrates on the grate.

Then Barnabas turns and gets right in my face. He grips my shoulders with his claws. "You are not to blame for the death of your son," he says with stern intensity. "Your former bound was mentally ill. You declared for her because it was your duty. She was from a good line, and she would make the Ashmoors stronger. No one knew of her mental illness—her family hid this from you. They hid it from everyone. Her parents knew she was unfit as a bound because she frequently went off her planned treatment and could be dangerous to herself and others. She was the reason for the death of your son. She killed herself and him in the process. I blame her parents for that tragedy as should you. They wanted so badly for their family to be joined with the Ashmoors that they took a risk they shouldn't and now they've lost their daughter and grandson in the process. She'd still be alive if instead they'd taken her treatment seriously and helped her by getting her the care she needed instead of pretending it wasn't happening. None of us could properly help her because none of us knew the extent of her illness."

Then Barnabas points a claw in my face. "And that human female you've impregnated, she is your true bound. I have come to know her, as has the staff. None of us care that she will be bringing human genes into your line. And you should not care either. If any of those assholes in the rest of aristocracy care, cut them off. What matters is that Charlotte Cruz will be a good mother to your offspring, and she loves you more than life itself. She has learned everything she can about our heritage, and I believe she cares for this manor and our traditions as much as we do. She is kind and loving toward the staff and we all respect her. I will not tolerate you treating her incorrectly."

This is wholly unexpected. My butler has never, in all the

years we've worked together, raised his voice at me or spoken to me this way. He is always professional and deferential. I have often heard his voice turn sharp when he gives direction to others outside of my office, but never towards me.

"You are the head of the Ashmoors," Barnabas reminds me. "You decide what the rules are. If any of those assholes arrive here tonight for the annual Fire Ball and try to treat Lady Ashmoor as anything less than her due, the staff will see them out. And if that Hyrrokin is a Viscount, a Marques, or a Fire-Baron, then so be it. They're out on their ass."

I grin at his savagery.

"We want her as your bound. We call her Lady Ashmoor on purpose, instead of fire-baroness, because it was obvious from the moment she arrived how you felt about her. I promised the Dowager on her death bed that I would protect you. I am protecting you right now by telling you the truth, even when it's hard to hear. You need to publicly declare for Charlotte and make her your bound in front of the citizens of Tarvos. It is the only way she will be fully accepted. You've impregnated her and now you need to let her know that you love her."

I find I am enjoying this version of Barnabas. "I will declare for her tonight at the Fire Ball, in front of everyone," I tell him.

"Good," he answers. A smile tugs at his lips. "Good."

18

CHARLOTTE

Tonight is the Fire Ball at Ashmoor Manor.
I'm going to show up to the biggest social event of the season pregnant and unmated. And on Tarvos, this is a big deal.

I have no idea how many of our guests know Thayne is the father of my baby. I think all of them? After that terrible vid I watched last night, where some of the aristocracy banded together to decry a human as a fire-baroness, I know that many of them will never accept me. I'm assuming the fact that I'll be at the ball as Thayne's pregnant ward that he hasn't even bothered to publicly declare for won't help matters.

It makes me want to hide out in my room and let the party continue on without me.

I can't do that. Can I?

Don't let the haters get you down, Rebyka said to me this morning. *I'll be there at the ball and I'm bringing my flask, this time it will be filled with extra dark Traq for fortification.*

I laugh at her remark and continue to ready for the event.

What's sad about these recent public attacks on the net, (none of which I've responded to) is that now that I've been living here for four months, I feel comfortable. I no longer feel like the visiting ward; I feel like this is my home.

Thayne's aunt has stopped by the manor for lunch and for 'garden chat' three different times. She likes what I've done with my little corner of the greenhouse. I've been with her to visit her daughter and grandchildren. The Strikestone lodge is my favorite place to visit and I've been there several times for meet ups with all the other human females who live on Tarvos. We've become our own tight-knit club.

Grimwall encourages me to change up the dowager's suite any way I want, to add my own personality. But I feel I can't yet because this is a bound suite and I'm not Thayne's bound. I'm just the female who carries his offspring and is technically still his ward. I believe he truly cares for me and is attracted to me, but I still think he's not ready for more. Which makes me sad.

We've only had real, penetrative sex that one night, when he got me pregnant. I sleep in his bed every night and he continues to give me mind-blowing orgasms, but he doesn't have actual sex with me. It makes me wonder if he won't cross that line because he doesn't love me?

It's difficult being in this in between place, not knowing the outcome of my future or if the man I love loves me back. Will I be able to stay here and raise my child alongside Thayne, or will I end up giving birth and needing to move out on my own and Thayne gets visitation rights?

"I'm so excited about the Fire Ball," Milli exclaims as she enters with a tray of refreshments and snacks. "It's the first one I get to see live, usually I just watch the arrival of all the royals, the nobility and the celebs later on the vid channels, but this time I'm here where all the action is happening."

This event is a big deal for the staff, as well as the citizens of Tarvos. Paparazzi and representatives from the vid news channels are gathered along the cobblestone driveway and front steps of the manor, readying to catch the arrival of all the VIPs.

Everyone on Tarvos loves the annual Fire Ball at Ashmoor Manor. The staff are a frazzled mess, having planned this event out for the last few months. Grimwall has been in charge of the whole thing and she looks exhausted. I've helped all I could, but I'm just learning. Hopefully, if I'm still here, each year I'll get better and better and be able to help more.

Milli looks at my face as she sets down the tray. "What's wrong?"

"Oh, I don't know...I just...I just don't know about my future," I admit, placing a hand on my tight stomach. The baby started kicking yesterday and I feel closer to him already. "I worry sometimes that after I give birth I won't be able to stay here and I'll need to take the baby and move out."

"But legally you are his bound," Milli says, confused. "You're not planning on staying here? I don't understand."

Tears form in her eyes and now I feel like shit. Sometimes I forget how invested the staff are in our lives. This doesn't just effect Thayne, the staff would be hurt too, not having the Ashmoor children in the manor. "I...I just don't know how I'm going to live with a man who doesn't love me. A man who holds half of his heart from me. A man who refuses to publicly declare me as his. I'm going to this Fire Ball tonight as only his ward and yet I'm pregnant with his child. How does that even work?"

She purses her lips and glances at the connecting door, "but you sleep with him every night. You two have dinner together every night. You message constantly. You seem...mated. I'm confused."

"I'm confused too. I'm far enough along in the pregnancy that I'm showing. So I'll walk into the ball and what do I say to everyone when they ask who the father is? Do I say yes, it's Thayne? Is he going to introduce me as his ward or as his bound?"

"You haven't spoken of this yet with Lord Ashmoor?" she says, aghast.

I bite my lip. "No, I was too scared of what he'd say. And he hasn't brought it up himself."

She blinks at me, totally at a loss for words.

And right then there's a knock on my door. Lorki shows up with her team and she looks very excited to get me ready for the event of the season. "I've gotten to know you well, and I think I've figured out what looks best on your human body and how to emphasize all your attributes. You are a beautiful female and I feel very lucky to have been able to dress you. Please accept this as my way of saying thanks. I've managed to get for you the latest dress from Lior Haute Couture and your jewelry will be again from the Ashmoor estate. I know white is your favorite color," she beams.

I glance at the garment on the rack and bite my lip. Do they even know that this looks like a wedding dress? I try not to laugh. She has no idea. I can't ruin this for her. She thinks she's found a special dress for the Fire Ball and crafted in a way I'll like. And it really is beautiful.

"Do you realize that now that I'm the stylist for the new human Lady Ashmoor, and after you wore that dress to the auction, I'm more popular than ever?"

"Really?"

"Yes. Now try this on."

I place a hand over my baby bump. "But.."

"Don't worry, I found a way to work around that."

I stand behind the screen and try on the dress, which is worn in two parts. There's a very short, embroidered top that pushes my breasts up and is lined with a light dusting of soft, downy white feathers. Then right under my breasts the dress loosens and flows in drapes of soft white fabric down over my stomach and along my hips and down to brush the tips of my toes. I notice when I move it opens in the front to expose a leg. I step out and Lorki helps me to fasten it in the back and they all look at me and sigh with delight.

And I really like it too. It's comfortable and sexy and classy at the same time. It's sadly, a wedding dress I would've picked out for myself.

Then they take if off of me and spend two hours primping me before putting it back on again—this time with white, low-heeled pumps I requested because it's getting harder to stand in high heels now that I'm pregnant. I figure any day now my ankles will start to swell.

Thayne is next door getting ready too. But he doesn't take as long as I do. He tried knocking on the door an hour ago, wanting in but Lorki shooed him away saying she wasn't done with her "magic" and to come back later. But now I'm done.

I step out of the suite and turn when Thayne meets me in the hallway outside both of our rooms. I stare at him from horns to toe and my heart almost stops in my chest. I love his edgy, scary handsomeness. I can never get enough of his shiny horns and the wafts of smoke from his nostrils. His pointy tail looks almost sharp this evening. His huge bare feet tipped with silver claws seem bigger, peeking out from the bottom of his perfectly tailored black trousers. Somehow his chest is harder and wider, and I swear I can already see his shaft swelling in his trousers.

I want it. Now.

He steps forward and takes my hand and says with a rough voice, "You are beautiful, inside and out."

And then I realize that Thayne has accepted me all along. He doesn't want anything from me besides my company and my... love? And well, my naked body in his bed, which is perfectly fine. He always thought I was sexy, from the moment he met me. He protected me and cared for me, while still giving me free will and choices. All he's ever wanted is me, but he thought he wasn't ready for another bound. He thought he was a sleaze for wanting an underage girl. I hope with all my heart he knows how wrong he is.

I decide it's time to kick things up a notch. I want this man and I need to make him mine. So I reach out and finger his sash and stand on my tip toes and whisper in his ear, "Now that I've seen how handsome you look for the ball, I want to warn you that there's no way I'm going to be able to keep my hands and mouth off your cock tonight. I'm going to sit on top of you, ready to sink down and fill myself with your shaft and ride you hard. If you don't want any of that you'd better avoid sleeping with me tonight."

He clears his throat and holds out his arm. I rest my hand on the crook of his red elbow. We walk down the hallways together and I hear the sound of voices. We take another turn and the entire staff of Ashmoor is lined along the hallway and down either side of the steps leading down to the grand foyer.

"Oh my gosh."

And then they all begin cheering and clapping for us. Oh gods they're going to make me cry and ruin my make up.

Thayne walks us along the procession and I smile and nod at all these beings I've grown so close to. I feel like a changed person. I used to be quiet and shy. I liked talking with people, but I never let them in close. And I didn't like confrontation, but now I can confront Thayne in a heartbeat. I'm not the same person who fell for the lies of Maya and her family. I opened myself to Jaden and Maya, only to be slapped down. But I'm proud of myself that I got right back up and made new friends. Better friends.

I make it down the stairs and then the party really starts. The grand foyer has transformed into a glittering reception area. The front doors swing open and Thayne and I stand inside, greeting everyone who arrives. This is much more intense than when I first met the staff or the VIPs at the charity auction.

Important beings exit their vehicles on the cobblestone driveway, to the delight of the paparazzi. Then they grandly ascend the front stairs and arrive at the entrance. I meet everyone there, including The President of Tarvos and his bound. It's crazy. I just keep smiling and shaking hands as Thayne introduces me to everyone simply as Lady Ashmoor. I'm happy to see Gurcil and her family. Avery Hellstone also arrives with her bound, Hannibal, along with her new best friend, the female who is the Secretary of Defense.

After smiles, handshakes and small talk they all move past me and continue down the hall to the glitzy ballroom. And then the whole vibe changes because I now see the same group of both male and female Hyrrokin who produced that terrible vid I saw last night, are entering the grand foyer.

I hear my name spoken with derision. Others continue, "…and she's pregnant with his offspring. How can he have impregnated a human?"

"Well, he hasn't declared for her, so I assume he doesn't really want her either? It was a mistake?"

"Where is she? I want to let her know exactly how I feel about her."

I step back, ready to run upstairs.

But right then, several things happen at once.

"It's the queen," I hear a crowd of beings exclaim. "The queen is here? I didn't know the Queen of Tarvos was arriving, she never comes to the Fire Ball."

I see out of the corner of my eye Thayne directing a team of Hyrrokin security to carry off and kick out the group of well-dressed and very angry nobles from the Fire Ball who were formerly insulting me. And…and the Queen of Tarvos has arrived and is standing in front of me, wanting to greet me?

I stare at her, speechless for a moment. "Rebyka?" I squeak. "Are you…?"

The queen takes my hand in hers. "Yes, my dear, I'm the Queen of Tarvos. And you're my friend, Lady Ashmoor."

Oh my gods. "I had no idea."

"I know." She leans close, "And bitch, this changes nothing between us. If you start acting weird around me, like everyone else does, I won't send you sweet fire-dates from my garden ever again."

My eyes widen. "Oh hell. I've got to have those dates. It's my biggest craving."

"Right? So don't change. I'm here to put a stop to this nonsense because you're human and to make sure they all accept you. Watch and learn."

And then Rebyka morphs into "the Queen". The way she walks, the sound of her voice and the nod of her head. She's so regal and imposing, I can't believe. It's like she's two different beings. I decide right then that she's the public persona- "the Queen" and to me, she's just Rebyka.

My friend snaps her fingers and requests a vid drone, letting the paparazzi and everyone nearby know she's about to make an important announcement. The space around us instantly becomes crowded and then very, very quiet.

"Lady Charlotte Cruz Ashmoor is my best friend," the Queen of Tarvos announces, "and I care about her very much. If anyone here, or amongst society, causes her a moment's distress that Hyrrokin will receive the cut direct from me and will no longer be considered worthy of reception by the queen or fire-society in general. Understood?"

There's an awed hush, and then a buzz of excited voices.

I meet her gaze with love shining in my eyes. For once, I have a real best friend. A being I can care for and count on. And I will cherish this, always.

And then Thayne returns to my side, frowning down at his cousin, "Rebyka." She gives him a mischievous grin and then instantly dismisses him as she turns to warmly greet a throng of subjects.

I suppose we're done with the formal greetings in the foyer because Thayne pulls me with him down the hall and into the main ballroom. I've been in here many times, walking around the grand, echoing space, imagining it was filled with parties just like this. It's impressive when empty but filled with the loud voices of this many Hyrrokin and their black horns, fancy clothes and flashes of flame—it's even more fantastical.

Thayne grabs a large mug of ale for himself off a passing tray.

And then I turn and see one last formally dressed Hyrrokin enter the ballroom behind us. He's alone and wears a sash across his chest similar to Thayne's.

"Bane!" The Fire Lord grins with delight and steps forward to greet the male who just arrived. "This is my brother, Sir Bane Ashmoor," he tells me. "Bane, this is my human ward, Charlotte Cruz Ashmoor."

Sir Ashmoor steps closer, examining us both critically. He sees how tightly Thayne holds onto my hand and I'm sure he's eyeing the swell of my pregnant stomach. He inhales and now I know he's doing what they all can—he's inhaling my scent and that of my child and he knows I carry Thayne's heir.

A muscle ticks in Bane Ashmoor's jaw. He's really pissed off. "I had no idea my brother was expecting a child," he says looking over at Thayne with an expression that could turn beings into stone, "and that his ward is legally his bound and yet he has not declared for her."

19

THAYNE

"Hold my ale," I tell my brother.

And then I pull my gorgeous, surprised female with me through the crowd and then up onto the stage of the grand ballroom. I'm about to apply a similar tactic to the one recently used by my sneaky second cousin, the Queen of Tarvos.

Everyone has arrived at the ball and now is the moment for me to make my announcement. I nod over at Barnabas who has been waiting for my cue. The music stops and the rest of the room darkens and a spotlight forms on both Charlotte and I on the stage. Voice projectors power online.

The room quiets and the most illustrious citizens on my planet turn to gaze at us. A small drone quietly floats in the air nearby, readying for live stream. This moment will be broadcast on all the vid news channels.

I take a deep breath and take Charlotte's hand in mine, bringing her forward to stand beside me. "Welcome to the one hundred and twenty-first Fire Ball at Ashmoor Manor," I announce to my guests. "The party is about to begin, but first there is one more announcement that needs to be taken care of. I need to let this female who is carrying my heir know how much I care for her."

There is an audible gasp from the crowd as I turn toward my bound and bend down on one knee before her, like I've been told human females prefer. I've studied human mating practices to learn how to make her dreams come true. She deserves this, and so much more. I plan on using the rest of my life to make her the happiest female that ever existed. Well, to the best of my abilities.

Tears form in Charlotte's eyes as she gazes down at me with a watery smile.

I take her hand in mine and gaze into her lovely human eyes and give her all the emotions I've kept bottled inside. "I love you, Charlotte Cruz Ashmoor," I say for the first time, in front of everyone. "You are my best friend and my bound. I knew you were my mate the moment I met you, but I've struggled to come to terms with my obligations as fire lord and the tragic death of my young son. I'd vowed to myself to never take on another bound or start a new family, because after my loss, I didn't think I was worthy of such a thing. I thank you for being patient with me and for being my friend and helping me to learn how to honor the past as well as move on. I look forward to my future with you as my partner, carrying on our Ashmoor traditions. And so I declare, in front of everyone assembled—Charlotte Ashmoor, will you accompany me to the courthouse to become my bound? Will you remain here with me as the mother of future Ashmoors?"

She clears her throat and responds loud and clear so everyone can hear, all the while staring lovingly into my eyes, "Yes Thayne, I would be proud to be your bound and live in this glorious manor with you and carry on Ashmoor traditions. And I love *you* Thayne Ashmoor, not only because I admire your dedication as the thirteenth Fire Lord of Ashmoor, but for the honorable Hyrrokin male that you are. You are my best friend, my lover and soon you will be the father of my children. Will you also do me the honor of becoming *my* bound?"

"Yes," I answer thickly, "yes, I would love to be your bound."

And then I take out the small black box that has been inside of my pocket all evening and I open it. Charlotte looks down at the sparkling ring and squeals with delight.

"I have learned that humans enjoy the exchange of rings as a powerful symbol of commitment," I say as I slip the glittering ring onto her finger. "This was my mother's favorite ring from the Ashmoor estate and I hope that you will enjoy it as my symbol of commitment to you and as a 'human wedding ring.'"

"I love it," she gasps, staring down in wonder at the ring I've placed upon her finger. "It's beautiful. Thank you so much."

And then I stand up and take her in my arms and kiss my pregnant bound in front of everyone. The crowd cheers and claps for us as she wraps her arms around my neck and kisses me in return. That damn drone circles around us, but I ignore it and place my claw behind her neck and hungrily thrust my forked tongue inside her mouth. I've very rarely kissed my female these last four months and I plan on making up for lost time.

Finally, we break free, both gasping for breath and I place my forehead against hers for a moment.

We should remain to talk, drink and dance the night away with our guests as they congratulate us on our declaration for each other. But I must have my bound, now. It's all her fault. She's the one who said she would have my cock in her mouth and body tonight. I am holding her to that promise. Besides, my cousin, the queen is in attendance tonight. She can easily preside over this ball in my stead.

I sweep my bound off her feet and carry her in my arms off the stage and down to the dance floor.

The crowd continues to cheer and whistle for us as they part. I march across the ballroom with my gorgeous, giggling bound in my arms. The music starts again behind us. And as I make it out the exit doors, I give a chin lift for my grinning brother. I know the illustrious guests will all forget about us in moments and carry on with their glamorous evening. Meanwhile I'll continue my evening upstairs, in our suite, with my bound.

"I'm hoping this means you're taking me to bed," my female purrs against my ear.

"Yes," I grunt, as I take the stairs two at a time, "I'm putting you on my cock right now."

"Okay," she breathes.

Then she laughs with delight as I race down the empty hallways with her and make it to our room in record time. I use a foot to kick open the door. And then I stomp over and toss her onto our bed.

The distant thump of music from the event below can be heard in our room, but this is no matter, up here it's just the two of us.

"Pants, off," she orders.

I quickly unbutton my trousers and pull out my thick red cock, which is uncommonly large, jutting up and ready for her. I hold it in my claw, stroking the length from root to tip, lingering on the seed leaking from the crown.

"Oh my gods," she sighs and sinks to the floor in front of me.

I grin because I know how much my pregnant female loves my cock and I'm ready to give it to her.

She immediately reaches for my hard shaft, gripping the base in her hand and placing her lips around the crown. In seconds she's taking all of me. I throw back my head and moan at the feel of those lush, hot lips moving exactly where I've always wanted. The reality is every bit as good as my dreams. I've been masturbating on a daily basis in my cleansing unit, but my own rough claw does not compare to the hot, silky slide of my female's mouth. I cup her head in my claw, guiding her human lips back and forth across my red cock.

I love watching her work so hard to take me as deep as possible. The in and out of my wet shaft through her lips is the most erotic vision of my life. I can already feel my balls tightening and that heady feeling of seed seeking release. I pull her off my dick and lift her up onto her feet. "I need you, now," I growl.

"I want to lick your balls," she pleads.

I pause. "Later. You need to be fucked."

And then she's on her back and I bend down and dig into layers of white skirt and discover her soaked underwear and tear it off. I'm already intimate with this perfect pussy. I've licked it at least a hundred times already and I'm an expert at providing satisfaction to my female. I haven't fucked her in months, but I've kept her satisfied. I know how much she loves hanging onto my horns or the end of my tail while she comes. She also particularly enjoys the attentions of my forked tongue on her clit. I will give her all of that this evening, several times over.

I've taken the entire week off and we are staying in bed fucking. The staff have already been ordered to leave meals for us on trays outside our door and to only knock if someone is bleeding or the mansion is on fire, other than that we are to be left alone.

This first time will be quick, but we'll have plenty of time later to linger. I want to spend hours bringing her to orgasm just from sucking and pinching her nipples. I want her on top of me. I want to take her from behind. I want to fuck her on every surface in this suite. Especially on the rug in front of the fireplace.

What she wants most of all right now is my cock deep inside of her. This is what I want too. I place my claws on her meaty thighs and my knees on the bed and I'm between her legs in an instant, with my trousers still around my hips. "I can't wait," I snarl. I reach down and part her seam, testing for wetness and discover just how slick and primed my bound is for me.

She grabs my cock, trying to place me at her sopping entrance. "Fuck me. Fuck me right now."

I sink partially inside of her, and we moan at the same time. Her breasts have grown larger, and I've learned that her nipples are even more sensitive than usual. I bend down, mindful of her pregnant belly, and suck on one tempting pink nipple and then move to the other and she gets even more slick. I shift my stance on the bed and sink further inside of her. Her hips loosen and her legs adjust their angle and then I slide again, and I bottom out and fill her up completely. My full length, clenched by her hot grip.

"So wet, so hot. I can't believe how tight and perfect you feel."

I lose control immediately and start pounding inside of her. I lift her legs higher, and I gaze down at her swollen stomach and watch as her teats jiggle as I plow in and out. And I know I'm not going to last long. But I refuse to release until she's right there with me.

"Touch yourself," I order. "I need you to come with me."

She wedges her tiny hand between us and fingers her clit as I continue to slide in and out of her. It's exactly what she needs. "Oh, Thayne," she gasps and grabs for my tail and squeezes the tip. "Oh, I'm..." She's tensing, getting close.

And then I feel her tighten around me as her orgasm crashes through her. Her back arches and I hold on, fighting to stay inside of her as I come harder than I've ever come in my entire life. A roar tears out of my throat. It's so hard and so long I swear I see spots of black. I jet the last drop from my balls and then do my best to catch myself and not fall on top of her.

"I love you," I gasp.

She cups my face between her hands. "I love you too," she laughs, then reaches behind me and grabs my ass. "Now, more sex."

And I give my female exactly what she wants.

EPILOGUE
THAYNE

O*ne year later*

I'M ABOUT to walk past the front foyer, but I pause at the sound of the knocker, curious to see who has arrived. Charlotte is already standing there with the porter as the door opens. I do not have any appointments, so I have no idea what Hyrrokin would be knocking on our door today.

The porter steps aside and I see a familiar-looking older female standing on the threshold. She meets my gaze from across the space. "I am here for a surprise inspection from the Department of Children and Families to check on the security and safety of your underage human ward."

My jaw drops open. Oh hells. I give Barnabas an accusing glare. Why didn't he stop this from happening?

I step forward to join Charlotte at the front door. The lawyer's eyes land on my female's slightly swollen belly. She is already pregnant with our next offspring. And our sleeping infant son, Targen Ashmoor, is in my arms.

"Good morning," my bound says, "welcome to Ashmoor manor. I am Charlotte Cruz Ashmoor and this is my bound, Thayne Ashmoor."

The lawyer lets out a dramatic gasp of surprise. "You birthed his offspring?"

How can she not know? Our union was the topic of conversation on all the vid channels and across the net for many moon cycles before finally dying down. "Yes. Charlotte Cruz was not a child, as you'd first claimed, and instead she was an adult on New Earth. I brought her back with me and made her my bound. She is now the Fire-Marchioness of Ashmoor. You may refer to her as Lady Ashmoor."

Charlotte places a soft, tiny hand on my forearm, "Lord Ashmoor is not at fault. I took advantage of him. I literally climbed into his bed one dark and stormy night during the worst of the rainy season. He'd been drinking a lot of fire-alcohol."

I roll my eyes at this remark.

Charlotte makes eye contact with Grimwall and gestures for her to come forward. In minutes the harsh lawyer is invited off the doorstep by my suddenly gracious housekeeper and offered brunch in the dining hall. The lawyer sputters a denial at first but then quickly agrees when someone mentions fresh fire-scones.

I adjust my sleeping son in my arms and come along, interested to discover the outcome of this new plan.

My staff pulls out all the stops. I watch in amazement as the porters, the chef and even Barnabas, all work in unison to charm this lawyer. Soon the older female is holding my infant son in her arms while nibbling on fire-scones and laughing at jokes I did not know Grimwall even knew.

Eventually I discover the lawyer's name is Maykel, and that she loves babies and has five grandchildren of her own. This is definitely more information than I needed to know. But, I open up to her. "My oldest child was Wylik Ashmoor, who passed away several years ago. My next two offspring are half-human, half-Hyrrokin, one of whom has not been born yet, and they are indeed my heirs. I think it is good for the Ashmoors, to have new blood and new ways brought in, to shake things up." I smile at my human bound. "My bound has decided that each year we will celebrate Wylik's birthday. She makes sure that his pics are prominently hung up on the walls next to the pics of our other offspring."

She takes my hand. "We will never forget him," she agrees.

"Well," Maykel finally stands, handing back my son to me, dusting off crumbs from the fire-scones she's eaten. "It looks like everything is fine here. I'll send in my report tomorrow to the Department of Children and Families and close this case. Charlotte Cruz is now twenty-one years old and therefore an adult. She is no longer your ward, and you are no longer her guardian. Thank you for the hospitality and the ability to meet your beautiful son. I wish you and your family the best."

And then the female leaves, waving happily, holding a large basket of wrapped fire-scones and bottles of Ashmoor wine in her arms.

I meet Charlotte's gaze and take her hand in mine. "Did you hear that? You are no longer my ward."

"And you are no longer my guardian," she laughs.

I squeeze her hand. "But you are instead the love of my life."

She kisses my claw. "And you are mine too," she breathes. "Always."

THE END

I HOPE you enjoyed the story!
Want Sir Bane's romance? Order His Human Stalker!

I SUFFER from resting bitch face (RBF).

It's sad but true. As a result, I turn people away. I'm not exactly bubbly and friendly.

This is probably why my lonely job as a private investigator is perfect for my skill set. Usually, I'm very good at what I do. I get the job done and move on. But my latest assignment has thrown me for a loop. The satanic-looking Hyrrokin biologist I've been tracking has gotten under my skin. Sir Bane Ashmoor has become much more than a job. Through my telescopic lens, I can literally see my future unborn children in his deadly eyes.

I'm full-on stalking this monstrous guy as he charts the migration of fire-beasts, spending countless *unbillable* hours in the wildlands, watching his every attractive move. What is wrong with me?

When I trip and break my ankle my hot target finds me with my ass in the dirt, doing the full-on ugly cry. And he lifts me in his massive red arms and carries me back to his tent! He's caring for me and I think he really likes me. Basically, it's a dream come true.

But what happens when Bane discovers he's brought his stalker home?

And he finds out who I really am, what I really do and who I work for?

cries

ABOUT THE AUTHOR

Michele Mills lives in California and leads a life of quiet, G rated desperation with her husband and two sons. In an attempt at a fulfilling, R rated inner life that does not include Disney movies and Nickelodeon; Michele reads and writes filthy romance and, well...filthy romance. And she wouldn't have it any other way.

ALSO BY MICHELE MILLS

Alien Bounty Hunters
Kroga's Bride
Rayzor's One
Joyzal's Prize
Kayzon's Wish
Syrin's Mate
Zhoryan's Game
Daxon's Hostage
Kroga's Redemption
The Alien Bounty Hunters Series: Books 1-8

Monsters Love Curvy Girls
His Human Nanny
His Human Surrogate
His Human Assistant
His Human Organizer
His Human Ward
His Human Stalker

Monster Bites
Her Alien Priest
Her Alien Ghost

The Fever Brothers
Mean Right Hook
Big Bad Claws

One Big Bite

The Swirl - Reverse Harem Romance
Cyborgs' Claim
Warriors' Claim
Gladiators' Claim

Battle Beasts - Alien Fantasy Romance
The Vandal and the Virgin

The Catastrophe Series
Die For You
Kill For You
Live For You

'In the Stars' Series
The Alien Assassin's Stolen Bride
Caught Between Two Blue Aliens

Lightning Source UK Ltd.
Milton Keynes UK
UKHW020148140522
403009UK00009B/1106